D1809447

SWEET IS DANGER

Set in 19th century Northumberland, this novel tells the story of seventeen-year-old Caroline, who is being pressurised by her family and their circle of friends to marry a dour young clergyman. She is also attracting the attention of a dashing baronet; however Caroline is stubbornly spurning the advances of both men. Her thoughts find a welcome distraction when rumours circulate that the Midnight Horseman has been sighted on Cullaton Moor. Is he the ghost of a hanged highwayman? A vicious vagabond? A handsome avenger? The headstrong, fanciful Caroline is determined to discover the truth and ventures out alone on to the moor at night; a foolhardy action which leads her into a world of espionage, adventure and romance . . . . .

SWEET IS DANGER

Hugh Roxburgh

ARTHUR H. STOCKWELL LTD.
Torrs Park   Ilfracombe   Devon
Established 1898
www.ahstockwell.co.uk

British Library Cataloguing-in-Publication Data.
A catalogue record for this book is available
from the British Library.

All the characters in this book have no existence outside the
imagination of the author, and have no relation whatsoever to anyone
bearing the same name or names. They are not even distantly inspired
by any individual known or unknown to the author, and all incidents
are pure invention.

ISBN 0 7223 3584-9
Printed in Great Britain by
Arthur H. Stockwell Ltd.
Torrs Park   Ilfracombe
Devon

Contents

Chapter One

The warm sunshine of a summer afternoon in the year 1814 poured down from a cloudless sky on the mellow grey walls and tall chimney stacks of Ullingham Grange, a rambling old manor house in a secluded hollow some three miles outside the little Northumberland town of Emberhope. Within the bright, cream-walled drawing room of the Grange sat two ladies. The one in the chair by the fireplace, working with impassive calm at the piece of needlework she held up in front of her, was Mrs Allen, the wife of Mr George Allen, the owner of Ullingham Grange. She was a tall, upright, handsome woman of early middle age, with smooth, brown hair, pale blue, rather chilly, eyes and a thin, severe mouth. The other, much younger, lady who was sitting on the hard-looking pink and green striped settee nearby, quietly busy over her work basket was Harriet the Allens' only child, a pretty, fair-haired, blue-eyed girl of eighteen.

Each lady pursued her separate task as though unaware of the other's presence and the only sound in the room came from the gentle tick of the ornate ormolu clock on the mantelpiece.

But at length, becoming bored with the prolonged silence Harriet paused in her work, and after studying her mother furtively for a few seconds, took the plunge. "Mama." Her small, childish voice broke upon the silence with startling suddenness. "Mama, shall we be going to Harrogate this autumn?"

"Harrogate, child!" exclaimed Mrs Allen. "I do not know. Your father has not made up his mind about it yet, so I cannot say."

"But have you, Mama?" Harriet pressed in honeyed tones.

Mrs Allen glanced sharply at the pair of big, blue eyes which gazed innocently up at her. "It is entirely for your father to decide," she replied stiffly. "You know I never try to influence him. If he wishes to go to Harrogate you may be sure I shall put no obstacles in his way."

"I do hope we shall go," Harriet murmured with something of a sigh. It is so dull in the country now. We have not danced since the ball Sir James Reddaway gave and that's nearly two months ago," she ended plaintively.

A frown crossed Mrs Allen's face and she uttered an exasperated 'tut'. "You really are excessively provoking, Harriet!" she snapped peevishly. "You must try to be a little less frivolous! There are other things to occupy yourself with besides parties and balls. You seem to forget that a high standard of accomplishment is expected of a girl in your position," she pointed out, pausing to regard her daughter. "You will not always live in this house, I hope, Harriet."

Subdued not a little by this lecture, Harriet hastened to make amends. "I shall try to be a good wife when I am married, Mama," she promised. Then, as the vision of the gay ballroom crossed her mind again, she added plaintively to herself "But I should like to enjoy myself a little first."

Unhappily this remark reached her mother's ears and she rounded upon her. "Oh — I have no patience with you, Harriet! Anyone would think you lived in a convent to hear you talk! Do you want to be dancing every night?"

"Oh, no, I did not mean that, Mama!" Harriet assured her hastily; but then, inspired by a sudden idea, she added naively "But if I do not go out I shall never meet any young men, Mama."

Poor Harriet's logic had quite the reverse effect to that which she had intended it to have. "Harriet, how vulgarly you talk!" Mrs Allen cried. "I do not mean you to throw yourself in the way of every young man you meet. That would be most undignified. Besides, a girl in your position does not need to. You are more fortunate than your cousin. With your advantages you can afford to be more particular."

"I haven't met anyone here I'd like to marry."

"Why — there are some charming young men in our circle! The two Digby boys and Augustus Heston-ffolliott and young Tom Hawley, all of them most eligible!"

"Oh, the Digbys are so dull and serious! I vow I never know what to say to them! And Augustus Heston-ffolliott is so odiously conceited!"

"Hoity-toity! I was not aware that you were so fastidious!" her mother scoffed. "However perhaps you have someone else in mind — Tom Hawley, for instance," she suggested, with a quiet smile.

Harriet turned her face away hurriedly for she could feel her cheeks glowing. "Oh, Tom Hawley is a horrid young man! He is so presumptuous! I cannot endure him!"

This was neither fair nor true. Harriet admired young Mr Hawley very much and she dared to hope that her feelings were reciprocated.

But she knew that if her mother guessed the state of affairs she would give her no peace till she had got her married.

"Since you are so hard to please it would be useless to offer you a baronet?" Mrs Allen inquired.

"A baronet!" Harriet looked up in surprise. "Do you mean Sir James?"

"Naturally."

"Oh, no, Mama." Harriet's voice died away and she picked up her sewing.

"Why not?" Her mother's tone was brusque. "He is a charming man and would be an excellent match for you. I have often thought of it. I cannot comprehend why he has not married. He must be nearly thirty now."

"I — I think he is in love with someone else," Harriet said in a low voice, not looking up from her work.

Mrs Allen dropped her sewing into her lap and stared at Harriet in astonishment. "With someone else! Sir James!"

"Yes, Mama."

"With whom, pray?"

"Caroline."

Mrs Allen was momentarily at a loss for words. "Caroline!" she repeated in an incredulous voice, at last. "Caroline! Oh, that's ridiculous! Sir James would never dream of it!"

"Well, he seems to admire her very much."

"Oh — it would be out of the question for Sir James to marry a girl who has neither position nor a fortune of her own."

"He was most attentive to her at the Knoxs' last week," Harriet argued. "He sat beside her almost the whole evening. I know everyone remarked on it."

"No doubt. But he probably paid her unusual attention out of kindness of heart because he did not want her to feel left out. I can see nothing in that," her mother stated certainly.

"Yes, Mama, perhaps you are right," Harriet conceded without conviction.

"Now if it had been the new rector of Cullaton I might have believed you," her mother went on. "He has been paying Caroline some attention, I have noticed, and I should not be at all surprised if he made her an offer one day."

"What — Mr Lark?" Harriet exclaimed.

"Yes. And I should be very pleased if he asked her to marry him — very pleased."

"I'm sure Caroline doesn't care for him at all. He's such a tedious creature," Harriet asserted emphatically. "And I don't think Caroline would make a very good wife for a clergyman."

Mrs Allen slowly lowered her needlework and regarded Harriet with an expression of sternness. "What you think, my dear, and what Caroline likes is neither here nor there. She will be a very foolish girl if she refuses Mr Lark. He is a well-bred sensible sort of a man and will make her an eminently suitable husband. He has a steadiness of character and a firmness of will which recommend him much. Caroline needs a husband who will be able to control her. I have always considered her too headstrong and self-willed."

"Poor Caroline! I hope he doesn't ask her to marry him then!" Harriet sighed. "I couldn't bear the thought of her shut up with him all day, listening to his prosy old lectures!"

"You're talking very stupidly, Harriet," her mother rebuked her irritably. "I hope you aren't going to set Caroline against him."

"Oh, no, Mama, of course not!" Harriet assured her promptly. She bent her head over her work basket with a smile. "There won't be any need to," she murmured to herself.

Mrs Allen was about to reprimand her daughter for her pertness when her attention was diverted by the entry of her husband. A robust, broad-shouldered country squire, Mr Allen had a plump, clean-shaven face and a pair of kindly blue eyes which reflected a placid, good-natured disposition.

"Harriet wishes to know whether we shall be going to Harrogate this season," his wife began in a severe tone. "I said that you had not made up your mind yet. That is so, is it not?"

"Harrogate! Oh — er — no, I had not thought about it yet," he replied in an uncertain manner, strolling across to the hearth rug.

"Harriet is dissatisfied with the amusements we provide for her in the country" continued Mrs Allen aggrievedly. "She wishes to be taken to Harrogate so that she may be assured of dancing at least four evenings a week."

Mrs Allen was being exceedingly tiresome about a mere trifle and Harriet was heartily sorry she had ever mentioned the subject of Harrogate.

"Oh, no, Papa, I am not dissatisfied with the amusements we have here!" she protested. "I was only wondering whether we should be going for a little while as we did last year."

"Well — er — it is a little early to decide yet," her father said cautiously, unwilling to commit himself before he had heard what his wife had to say. "Your mother and I have not discussed the matter. But we shall do our best to please you, my dear," he promised, with a kindly smile.

"George, I will not have you indulging her!" his wife broke in in tones which made him tremble. "You are far too easy-going with both the girls. I do not know what is becoming of young people these days. They seem to be able to think of nobody but themselves."

She resumed her sewing, with a slightly offended air, and father and daughter exchanged surreptitious glances and Harriet hastily snatched up a handkerchief in front of her face to smother a giggle; and silence fell upon the room again.

Suddenly, with a violence which made the three of them turn and look up in startled surprise, the door was flung open and another very young, and extremely pretty, lady burst into the room with just the lack of thought for others that Mrs Allen had been complaining of a few minutes before. Taller and slimmer than Harriet, she had pale, delicate features and long, sweeping eyelashes drooping down over lovely, soft, grey eyes. Her light brown hair was bound up with a blue ribbon matching the sash of her sprigged muslin dress and long ringlets hung down on either side of her clear cheeks.

"Have you heard about the Midnight Horseman?" she burst out breathlessly, hurrying forward into the room, her eyes bright with excitement. "He was seen again last night!"

"Oh, Caroline, where was he seen? Who saw him?" Harriet demanded, jumping up from the settee.

"One of Farmer Blake's shepherds saw him at the crossroads on Cullaton Moor just before twelve o'clock," replied Caroline Berkley, Mr Allen's niece and ward.

"What was he like?" questioned Harriet eagerly.

"The man only caught a glimpse of him because he rode off before he could get close to him; but he said he was dressed all in black and was riding a big, black horse," her cousin told her.

Harriet clapped her hands together and looked up at the ceiling with an expression of delight. "Oh, how thrilling!" she exclaimed gleefully. "That's the third time he's been seen!" She turned to Mr Allen. "Papa, do you think he can be a ghost?"

"I do not!" the latter responded, with unexpected asperity. "It is probably some scoundrel who is using the legend of the spectral highwayman as a cloak for his lawless actions."

"But they did hang a highwayman at the crossroads once, didn't they, Uncle George?" interposed Caroline artlessly.

"Caroline! You forget yourself!" her aunt protested in scandalised accents. "That is not the sort of thing for a well-bred girl to talk about!"

Caroline blushed and turned and walked with downcast eyes to the window seat where she knelt, looking out into the garden.

"Do you think he is a highwayman then, Papa?" Harriet persisted.

"He may be," her father admitted, with a shrug. "But I thought we had got rid of that kind of a pest long ago. I have not heard of one for twenty years." He stopped abruptly and a thoughtful frown crossed his face. "And yet now I think of it — " He pondered a moment and then muttered to himself! "Yes, it is strange." He stared abstractedly at the carpet, ignoring the three ladies who were looking at him with puzzled expressions.

"What is strange, George?" his wife demanded impatiently.

Mr Allen raised his head slowly. "It has just occurred to me, my dear, that this mysterious horseman has been in the district nearly a fortnight now and yet there has been no report of any robbery or like misdeed," he said. "Now if he is here on criminal intent one would have expected him to have — well — displayed his talents — committed some felony by now. But he has apparently done nothing — not so much as robbed an orchard."

"Then I am certain he is a ghost," Harriet declared confidently.

"Well, whatever he is his presence in the district is most disturbing and the sooner something is done about him the better," Mrs Allen complained. "I consider it a disgrace that a man who is plainly bent on mischief should be permitted to roam the roads at night like this."

"We cannot be sure that he is bent on mischief," her husband objected mildly.

"Do not be absurd, George! How can it be otherwise?" Mrs Allen retorted brusquely. "The very fact that he only appears after dark is sufficient proof that he is not honest. It amazes me how the justices can be so negligent as to allow a desperate character like this to jeopardise the lives of the people whom it is their duty to protect," she concluded in a tone of severe disapprobation.

As Mr Allen was one of the county magistrates he was included in this forthright condemnation, and seeing in it a pretext for escaping from the drawing room, he said hastily "I think it would be as well, perhaps, if I went down to the town and made some enquiries about the man. There may be something I have not heard." And without waiting to hear his wife's views on this course of action, he left the room.

"That reminds me!" exclaimed Mrs Allen, as the door closed behind him. "I promised we would call on Mrs Knox this afternoon." She folded up her needlework and laid it carefully on top of the mahogany occasional table beside her chair. "Go and get ready, children; the carriage will be round directly."

Harriet and Caroline rose from their seats and followed her obediently out of the room.

Chapter Two

A few minutes later the carriage was jolting sedately along the road to Emberhope. Mrs Allen sat in solitary state facing the horses with Harriet and Caroline on the seat opposite. More reserved and more intelligent than Harriet, Caroline had much in common with her uncle, his quiet sense of humour, his interest in books, his love of the countryside in which he lived. Perhaps that was why he was almost fonder of her than he was of his daughter who was too boisterous for him; certainly he had never regretted bringing her to Northumberland when she had been left an orphan at the age of five.

As the carriage passed by the bystanders loitering on the bridge at the end of the town turned admiring eyes on the pretty couple inside in their high-crowned bonnets with dangling silk ribbons.

"A fine pair o' girls they are o' Mrs Allen," observed one old dame. "'Twon't be long afore some fine gen'lmen come asking for to marry them."

"Ah, Squire's lady learned them well. A proper 'ansum pair, 'tis not to be denied," her companion croaked sagely.

Unconscious of these friendly compliments, the cousins contemplated the familiar sights of the town; the uneven row of bow-fronted houses with flights of steps up to their hooded porches and the little shops with thick, greenish panes in their curved windows; the flock of geese marching in an ungainly procession across to the pond in the middle of the green in front of the imposing white facade of The Rose and Crown, the massive carthorses clumping ponderously up to the blacksmith's forge and the sunburned labourers who touched their forelocks as the carriage rumbled over the cobbled street.

Just beyond the church a lane turned off the main street. On one side of the lane stood the Rectory and a little further on the opposite side, stood Court House, so called because its creeper-covered walls had been built round a small courtyard. This was the residence of Sir James

Reddaway, the young baronet of whom Mrs Allen had been talking to Harriet a short time ago.

The carriage turned into the lane and a few moments later the three ladies were being received in the Rectory drawing room by Mrs Knox and her daughter, Charlotte. The wife of the Rector of Emberhope was an elegant, capable woman, whose commanding presence and assured voice earned her great respect in the parish. There was little that escaped her notice, whether it be the behaviour of the children in church or the interesting attention that young Mr Brown was paying pretty, little Miss Gray.

"Has the archdeacon returned?" Mrs Allen inquired when they were all seated.

"Yes, he arrived in time for dinner yesterday," Mrs Knox replied. "He was compelled to delay his return for another day owing to the great pressure of diocesan business. He met Sir James Reddaway in Durham and they were able to travel home together. Wasn't that fortunate?"

"The archdeacon must have been glad to have found such a congenial companion," Mrs Allen commented.

"Oh, yes, indeed! Such an interesting person, is he not? And yet — " Mrs Knox paused. The rumour, slight yet but disturbing enough, that the baronet appeared to be attracted by a certain young lady at Ullingham Grange had not escaped her inquisitive ears, and since she planned that Charlotte should one day be mistress of Court House, she felt that the rumour required investigation. "He is a strange man," she continued. "He is so reserved, his manner is so aloof, almost distant at times, as if he was reluctant to encourage really intimate friendships." She smiled thoughtfully to herself. "Perhaps that is why he is so intriguing. Do you not think so, my dear," she inquired abruptly, turning with an encouraging smile to Caroline.

The stuffy room and the dull conversation had lulled Caroline into a comfortable drowsiness, and she was quite unprepared for this unexpected question and hadn't the least idea what Mrs Knox had been saying. "Oh — yes — I mean — yes, I think so," she stammered, averting her face quickly.

But Mrs Knox did not fail to notice Caroline's confusion which only seemed to confirm what was being whispered about her in connection with the owner of Court House. "I declare I positively envy you young people having him for a partner in a dance!" she exclaimed gaily. "It makes me wish I was a girl again to watch him! Do you judge him a good dancer, Caroline?"

"I think so, ma'am, though I can hardly tell since I do not think I have danced with him above two or three times."

"I know Charlotte thinks highly of him as a dancer," Mrs Knox said. "I have often heard her praise him. Is that not so, Charlotte?"

Charlotte Knox, a haughty, languid beauty of three and twenty, did not even look up when her mother spoke to her. "Yes, Mama, he is a tolerable dancer," she answered unenthusiastically.

"I always think they make an excellent couple in the ballroom," her mother continued, not a wit put out by her apathy. "They are so well matched in height and they have such a perfect understanding of each other's steps." She broke off for a moment. "It will be interesting to see if our newest arrival is a good dancer. I mean Mr Lark, the new Rector of Cullaton."

"A most amiable young man!" Mrs Allen acknowledged warmly. "I was most favourably impressed by him when he was introduced to me. His manner is gentlemanly and respectful and in conversation he is sensible and interesting. He will be a welcome addition to our society."

"The archdeacon speaks highly of him," Mrs Knox said. "He has set about his work in his new parish with commendable energy and I am happy to see that he has already effected some much needed improvements in the parsonage at Cullaton. And I believe he means to look for a wife," she confided, with an arch smile. "Only yesterday he was complaining to me how lonely it was for him at Cullaton; and when I suggested that he needed a wife to look after him he said at once that he hoped it would not be long before there was a Mrs Lark." Her shrewd eyes seemed to dwell on Caroline an instant. "And if I am not mistaken he has already made his choice."

Harriet stole a glance at her cousin; but Caroline did not appear to be in the least bit interested in the projected matrimony of the Rector of Cullaton. She was gazing out of the window with a faraway expression on her face.

"She will be a very lucky girl whom he selects and it is to be hoped she will be sensible of her good fortune," Mrs Allen stated in her dogmatic way. "He has much to recommend him and he is not at all a bad looking man. Is he to be one of the party at Elmcross next week?"

"Yes. He told me he was looking forward to it very much. Harriet and Caroline will be there, of course?"

"Yes, they have both been invited."

"It should be a delightful party. Charlotte always enjoys going to Elmcross. Do you not, my dear?"

"Yes, Mama" came the reply, obedient and unemotional.

The conversation continued for a few minutes longer till Mrs Allen rose to take her leave. Harriet and Caroline rose too, with remarkable promptness, each with an inward sigh of thankfulness that the tedious visit was over; or nearly over; for as they all moved towards the door the sound of voices came to them from the hall.

"Ah, here is the archdeacon!" Mrs Knox cried, opening the door and leading the way into the hall.

The archdeacon, a tall, lean, angular man, with thick black hairy curling, bushy eyebrows and monstrous side whiskers, was talking in deep, authoritative tones to another clergyman in the window recess in the hall. As he turned and strode across the hall to greet Mrs Allen Caroline saw that his companion was the new Rector of Cullaton and she drew back and tried to hide herself behind the others.

"You will be glad to be home again, Archdeacon," Mrs Allen was saying. "You have had a busy time in Durham, I am sure."

"Yes, there is usually a great deal for me to attend to at the Castle," he assented, with a self-important bow. "I have just been telling my young friend here of some of the matters I discussed with the bishop," he went on grandly, indicating the Rector of Cullaton with a wave of his hand. "You know, Mr Lark, of course. He has lately been appointed to succeed Dr Merrilock at Cullaton.

"Yes, we have met several times already," Mrs Allen replied, moving towards the young clergyman with a gracious smile. "I hope you are comfortably settled at Cullaton by now, Mr Lark," she said to him.

Eager to draw himself to the notice of the ladies of Ullingham Grange, Mr Lark bowed with unusual ceremony as he shook hands with Mrs Allen. Not at any time an imposing man, being short and slight and having thin, sandy-coloured hair, a receding chin and solemn, lacklustre, brown eyes, he showed to even greater disadvantage beside the magnificent figure of the archdeacon; and Harriet had to look away hurriedly to hide the smile which she felt might at any second become audible in the form of an uncontrollable giggle if she went on looking at this unprepossessing, almost comical, young man.

"Thank you, ma'am," he began in a prim, slightly effeminate voice. "Yes, I am happy to be able to inform you that I am established in the Rectory at last. It has taken me a considerable time as I found it necessary to effect a number of alterations in the arrangement of the house. But I think I can say with confidence that I have now a residence in which I can receive my friends with the hospitality that they would expect of me." He paused to give his audience time to take this in. "I should deem it a favour, ma'am, if you would condescend to visit my simple abode on a day convenient to yourself so that you may view the improvements I have been so bold as to make."

Harriet was by this time biting her lips to bleeding-point in an effort to conquer the well-nigh irresistible urge to shriek with laughter.

"It will give me great pleasure to call upon you at Cullaton," Mrs Allen told him kindly.

"Thank you, ma'am. I am most obliged to you. I shall look forward to conducting you over my house with the utmost felicitation," he assured her in an earnest manner. "I need hardly say that my invitation is extended to your charming daughter and niece. You will bring Miss Allen and Miss Berkley with you, I trust?" he ventured, smiling gallantly at Harriet and Caroline.

"Certainly, Mr Lark. I know they will be delighted to come," Mrs Allen replied.

"How kind of you, ma'am!" the young rector exclaimed, his face lighting up with unwonted animation. "Having no female relations to apply to for advice, I have been compelled to rely on my own judgment regarding the furnishing of my residence and I am therefore anxious to know whether it will meet with the ladies' approval?" he explained, favouring the ladies present with an ingratiating simper.

"Are you not taking a grave risk, Mr Lark?" Mrs Allen observed drily.

"Oh, no, ma'am! I am most eager to have your expert opinion on my modest efforts!"

"Well, we will not be too hard on him, will we, Caroline?" Mrs Allen laughed, turning to Caroline.

Caroline's response was the briefest and chilliest of smiles and Mrs Allen moved on towards the front door with Mrs Knox and the archdeacon.

The girls followed them and Caroline found that she was no longer able to ignore the Rector of Cullaton who was sidling up to her. "I hope you will persuade your aunt to pay her visit soon," he whispered, affecting a most genial smile.

"I am sure she will wish to call upon you as soon as it is convenient to her," Caroline told him politely.

"You will accompany her too, I hope," Mr Lark entreated, thrusting his beaming face closer.

"If she wishes me to," Caroline answered coolly.

"I shall look forward to that day with great pleasure," he declared, undaunted by her lack of enthusiasm. "We shall be meeting at Mrs Digby's house also, I believe?"

"Yes, sir. My cousin and I have been invited."

"I am delighted! We shall be able to continue our little chat there," he murmured in a conspiratorial whisper.

However this evoked no response from his fair companion; and though she had to submit to being escorted down the steps and handed into the carriage by Mr Lark she barely touched his proffered arm and acknowledged his courtesy with but the slightest nod of her head; and since she was staring intently out of the opposite window as the carriage moved off down the drive she missed the look of deep admiration in Mr Lark's eyes as he gazed after her.

Chapter Three

The legend of the Midnight Horseman, whose name had created such a commotion in the Grange drawing room, dated back to the middle of the eighteenth century when a highwayman had attempted to rob two farmers returning from market across the moor one October night. Being in an inebriated, devil-may-care condition, they simply burst into roars of laughter when challenged, and the highwayman was so taken aback that he was unable to dodge the terrific clout that one of the farmers dealt him with a knobbly stick. With their captive trussed up in the back of the cart, the revellers went on their way, in high glee and noisier than ever.

But their triumph was short-lived. On the eve of his execution the highwayman vowed that he would haunt the moor till he had had his revenge. Undeterred by this, the farmers continued to cross the moor. But something always went wrong; an axle broke, the horse went lame, they got lost in the mist. Then came the crowning disaster. While crossing the moor late one night they suddenly found their way barred by a spectral horse and rider. Their own horse took fright, careered off into the heather, breaking its neck and tossing its passengers in cursing confusion into the prickly heather. Never again did the farmers cross Cullaton Moor after nightfall, declaring that it was undoubtedly haunted by the highwayman's ghost.

That this was true the superstitious rustics were only too ready to believe; and the alleged appearance of a phantom rider revived the old story, and nowhere more strongly than in the little village of Cullaton which lay just below the moor to the southeast.

Because of the remoteness of its situation Cullaton had not grown into a community of any size or affluence. Humble dwellings were ranged on either side of its broad street, and half-way up, facing the pump and the stocks, stood the church, its rugged walls weatherworn and lichened, its squat tower the haven of wheeling and cawing jackdaws.

Only the imposing pair of wrought-iron gates at the head of the street and the large Elizabethan mansion in its broad acres of parkland beyond them saved it from complete obscurity; for Chollingford Hall was the seat of the Earls of Wrosthdale who for centuries had been lords of the manor of Cullaton.

This, then was the corner of England whither the Reverend William Lark had been directed by Providence to commence his labours as a parish clergyman. His boyhood had been spent in a remote village in Lincolnshire. Never having been a robust child, he had been coddled by indulgent parents and kept from all energetic pastimes like tree-climbing and rat-hunting. Not ungifted, he had devoted much of his time to the study of Latin and Greek authors so that he had come down from Oxford with commendatory testimonials from his teachers. Now at the age of twenty-six he had grown into a ponderous, narrow-minded intellectual, much filled with a sense of his own importance, fond of the sound of his own voice and sadly lacking in humour.

The Rector of Cullaton was one of the people furthest from Caroline's thoughts as she sauntered down the garden, basket in her hand and a faded, straw bonnet perched casually on her head, on the afternoon of the Elmcross dinner party. When she came to the rose garden she paused indecisively in the archway, contemplating the rose beds.

"Good afternoon, Miss Caroline."

The wheezy voice which addressed her from apparently nowhere made her turn with a perplexed smile; her face lit up as she perceived Benjamin Tullitt, Mr Allen's head gardener peering up at her over a rose tree a little way off.

"Good afternoon, Benjamin," she responded politely, going over to the bed where he was working. "You gave me quite a fright," she laughed. "I didn't know you were there."

"Ah, I bin watching you quite a while now," Benjamin informed her, a mischievous grin lighting up his wrinkled, sunburned, old face. "But you be so much in the clouds that you never see'd me," he complained in a rasping, singsong voice.

"Oh dear! Well, I'm very sorry!" apologised the young lady in a gravely contrite voice which ill-matched the demure twinkle in her lovely grey eyes.

Benjamin Tullitt was a wizened, bent old man with watery, blue eyes, a stubbly chin, muscular arms and sturdy but very bandy legs. He was hard-working, kind-hearted and so honest that he would never shirk expressing his candid opinion no matter the consequences. He was distinguished in two ways; he had a rather unpleasant habit of spitting at regular intervals while he was working and he was the only person with whom Mrs Allen never tried to argue. Caroline and he had been firm friends ever since the day she had sneaked into the garden on her own soon after first coming to the Grange. She had come upon Benjamin unexpectedly as he turned the corner of the path, pushing a wheelbarrow. At the sight of the queer, weather-beaten man in worn clothes and battered straw hat the little girl stood rooted to the ground, staring at him with a mixture of horror and amazement. Then, just as she was on the point of turning round and scurrying back to the house, he smiled. She smiled back at him, doubtfully at first; but when he put down the barrow and asked her if she liked flowers the ice was broken; she trotted happily along beside him while he showed her the mysteries of his garden, till an anxious nursemaid came and took her back to the house.

That was the first of many visits that Caroline made to the garden to see Benjamin. She would stand beside him, helping him to gather fruit, and as a reward he would solemnly hand her an apple or pear which he had carefully selected for her.

Caroline stood watching the old man tying up the rose tree, till recollecting her errand, she said meekly "Please may I have some roses, Benjamin?"

"You may 'ave as many as you've a mind to, my dear," he answered, straightening up and pulling a villainous-looking, horn-handled knife from his breeches pocket.

"Oh, no, don't bother! I can get them!" Caroline protested, delving in her basket for the scissors.

But the old fellow was not to be put off and he stumped down the path to the big rose bed where he commanded her to make her choice.

When the basket was full Caroline lifted it up to her face to breathe in the delicate scent of the roses. "Aren't they exquisite!" she murmured rapturously. She put the basket down at her feet and turned away, with an upward gaze. "Oh, what a perfect day it is! It's all so quiet and peaceful!"

"Ah, but 'tis not so quiet after sundown!" Benjamin growled, with a gloomy shake of his head.

The happy, faraway look faded from Caroline's face and she stared at him in puzzled surprise. "After sundown! Why — what do you mean?" she demanded.

"Strange goings-on an' all," he muttered darkly. Then seeing her blank look, he whispered "You've not heard about the robbery then?"

Caroline's eyes grew round with astonishment and she uttered a tiny gasp. "Robbery! What robbery?"

Benjamin fingered the blade of his knife uneasily and bent down and chopped off a dead rose. "P'raps I didn't ought to 'ave said nothing," he muttered dubiously.

But Caroline's curiosity was thoroughly aroused by this time and she was not going back indoors till she had wheedled the whole story out of Benjamin. "Benjamin, please tell me about the robbery," she pleaded, stooping down and compelling him to meet her eyes. "I don't know anything about it," she added a trifle wistfully.

The old man looked up at her from beneath the tattered brim of his straw hat and surrendered to the irresistible appeal of the grey eyes. Casting a furtive glance behind him, he stepped up to her and whispered "Well, don't be telling no one, miss, but — " his voice sank almost to inaudibility, " — Court House was visited last night!"

Caroline jerked back, her eyes wide open. "Court House! Visited!" she gasped.

Benjamin nodded his head ponderously. "I 'eard two of the grooms speaking of it when I was down at the Crown this morning," he went on in the same mysterious whisper. "They was loading some oats in the yard and they didn't know I was there else they wouldn't 'ave spoke so loud, I reckon. I 'eard them say that a man had come in the night and broken into the 'ouse when all were abed."

"Did he steal anything?"

"I don't know. I didn't catch everything they said and I 'ad to slip away afore they finished talking in case they'd 'ave seen me. I were 'iding behind the pump," he explained, with a dry chuckle. "But I doubt but what Sir James wants it kept quiet. Fair wild he was about it and gave orders that none of the servants were to speak about it to anyone. I remember that 'cause one of the grooms told t'other not to be such a fool talking so loud."

"But why ever should Sir James want to do that?"

Benjamin shook his head and snipped off another dead rose. "Queer chap is Sir James," he commented cryptically. "A real rum 'un, I reckon."

They were silent for a few moments. A thoughtful frown wrinkled Caroline's brow as she watched the old gardener tidying the roses. Behind her frown her mind was considering an idea that had occurred to her. "Benjamin — " she hesitated, "Benjamin, have you ever seen the Midnight Horseman?"

The gardener's busy fingers stopped suddenly and he remained absolutely still for several seconds. Then he turned slowly round and looked up at her, his face expressionless. "No, Miss Caroline, I never seen 'im."

"I was wondering — do you think it might have been he who broke into Court House?" Caroline suggested.

"Maybe."

Caroline contemplated his bent back for a moment before plucking up courage to ask her next question. "Do you think — do you think he's a ghost?" she inquired timidly.

"I do not!" came the reply, so swift and curt that she was quite frightened and was momentarily silenced.

"Don't you believe in him at all?" she ventured at length.

"P'raps."

Benjamin was being extraordinarily unhelpful, but with a little coaxing Caroline felt confident that she could persuade him to be a shade more expansive. "What do you think he is doing here?"

The old man stood up and a flicker of a smile played over his cracked lips as he turned to her. "No I ain't seen 'im and I know nothing about 'im, my dear, so 'ow can I say what 'e's up to?" He spat and bent to gather up some dead flowers. "I don't know as 'ow I think 'e's up to anything as a matter o' fact."

"But don't you think it's a very strange thing for a man to do to ride about a lonely moor at night?" Caroline persisted.

"If 'e wants to ride on the moor at night there ain't no reason why 'e shouldn't, I reckon," Benjamin retorted coolly, "'e does no harm by that and I'm sure 'e's welcome to the 'ole of the moor if 'e likes."

"But what about the robbery at Court House?"

"Nobody said 'e done it," Benjamin pointed out. "If Sir James suspected the 'orseman why don't 'e say so instead of trying to 'ush it up." He straightened up again and faced Caroline. "It ain't a bit o' use you trying to get anything out o' me, my dear. I know no more nor you nor anyone else about the creature, so I can't 'elp you. The best advice I can give you is to forget about 'im altogether," he lectured, wagging an admonitory finger at her as he spoke. "Midnight riders ain't the sort of thing for pretty ladies like you to think about."

Caroline's face lit up with a merry smile and she gave a quiet, little chuckle. "I'm sorry, Benjamin. It was silly of me to have kept on asking so many questions," she apologised. "I had better take these in now," she said, picking up the basket of roses. "Thank you very much for helping me." And with a wave of her hand she ran gaily off up the garden.

In her bedroom later that afternoon, dressing for the dinner party, Caroline's mind went back to her conversation with Benjamin. What possible reason could Sir James have had for wanting to have the robbery at Court House hushed up? Surely he owed it as a duty to his friends and neighbours to warn them that there was a thief in the district. He couldn't have thought the incident not worth bothering about otherwise he wouldn't have been so angry about it and given orders to his servants that it wasn't to be talked about. Yes, that was very puzzling. Why this strange secrecy on the part of Sir James? Had he some particular reason for concealing the break-in?

Caroline shook her head helplessly and began to untie her hair. Dare she ask Sir James about the burglary, she wondered, as she drew a comb slowly through her ringlets? But she dismissed the idea almost at once. It would be foolish to attempt such a thing, she reflected, even if she got the opportunity to speak to him alone for a minute, which was most unlikely. He would probably consider it an impertinence on her part to meddle in his affairs and would simply snub her. No, Caroline didn't fancy the thought of quizzing that austere, taciturn man, for if his resentment was aroused he might be rather unpleasant. Still, it would be interesting to see how he reacted when she showed him that she knew what had happened at his home last night. And if he really had ordered his servants to keep the affair secret, it would be equally interesting to see how he justified his rather strange action. And after all, she argued, unable to repress her curiosity, what did it matter if he did snub her? She didn't care what he thought of her; and she wasn't desperately eager for his esteem. She smiled wickedly into the mirror and tossed her head defiantly. Yes, it might be worthwhile challenging him, if only she could find the courage to do it, for she realised she ran the risk of quarrelling with Sir James and perhaps making him her enemy too; and somehow, at the bottom of her heart, Caroline had an uneasy feeling that that might be an unwise thing to do.

Chapter Four

A number of the guests were already present when Harriet and Caroline were shown into the Digbys' drawing room at Elmcross, but Caroline noticed, as she glanced round the room, that Sir James Reddaway had not yet arrived. Mr Digby was standing on the hearth rug, discussing the prospects for the harvest with several of the gentlemen, and near one of the long windows Charlotte Knox was in conversation with a well-built, merry-eyed, young man, with fair, untidy hair, whom Caroline recognised as Tom Hawley.

Mrs Digby, a warm-hearted, unpretentious, little woman, hurried forward to welcome her guests from Ullingham Grange. "What a beautiful evening it is!" she exclaimed. "It has been such a splendid week! But we really do need a little rain now! The roads are becoming shockingly dusty!"

"The gardens need rain very badly," Harriet said. "The excessive heat makes the flowers fade very quickly. I declare Caroline is never without her watering can when she is in the garden!"

"Of course — you are a keen gardener, are you not?" Mrs Digby said, turning to Caroline with a kindly smile. "You must see my water lilies after dinner if it is not too cold. They have been excellent this year!" she exclaimed proudly.

"Oh, I should love to see them!" Harriet broke in, before Caroline had time to reply. "Can you see them from the window?" she demanded eagerly.

"Yes, you can just see the pond at the end of the lawn" her hostess told her.

She was going to add that the lilies looked their best in the daytime when they were fully open. But Harriet had already joined Charlotte and Tom Hawley; and as Caroline went on talking to Mrs Digby she could hear their noisy, light-hearted chatter in the background and she guessed that Tom was paying more attention to Harriet now than to Charlotte.

A minute or two later the guest for whom they had been waiting was announced and Mrs Digby left Caroline with her younger son, William, while she went with her husband to receive the newcomer. As she talked to William Digby Caroline took the opportunity to study the lean, stiff-backed, immaculately dressed gentleman to whom the Digbys were talking. Striking rather than good-looking, Sir James Reddaway wore the air of an ascetic, with his smooth, black hair, gaunt, almost haggard, features, thin lips and intense, dark brown eyes. He had the firm, brisk voice and assured bearing of a well-informed unsentimental man of the world; and as she watched him gravely talking to his host and hostess Caroline could not but feel that he was not a person to be trifled with, and her misgivings about her resolve to question him on the burglary at his house were renewed.

The entrance of the butler to announce dinner put an end to Caroline's reflections, and, to her inexpressible mortification, she found herself being taken into dinner by Mr Lark; and her cup was full when she found, when they were all seated, that she had Edward Digby, a dull, inarticulate youth, on the other side of her. Almost bitterly did she envy her cousin who was at Mr Digby's end of the table, in high spirits and obviously enjoying herself thoroughly. It was one of the rare occasions when Caroline let her feelings get the better of her; and finding she could neither silence nor ignore the loquacious bore on her right by entering into conversation with her tongue-tied companion on her left, she relapsed into sullen and, it must be admitted, ill-mannered silence. Charlotte Knox and Sir James who were sitting opposite also appeared little disposed to make much conversation, being content to listen with polite, if feigned, interest to the homely chatter of the hostess.

As she sat stifling her discontent and repressing an almost overwhelming urge to box Mr Lark's ears, Caroline suddenly became conscious of a pair of eyes studying her from the other side of the table. Glancing up quickly, she found Sir James Reddaway looking at her. His grave, inflexible features betrayed not the slightest change when their eyes met, nor did he, to Caroline's annoyance, remove his eyes from her. She returned his steady gaze unwaveringly for an instant; then she turned her head away, her chin tilted and her eyebrows lifted disdainfully; and in doing so, she missed the amused smile which hovered for a second on his face before he began to talk to his neighbour again.

Though remaining outwardly calm and doing her best to forget the tiny incident by engaging in a brisk discussion with Mr Lark on the advantages of country life, to that gentleman's immense gratification, Caroline could not easily subdue the tumult of indignation which surged up within her. The impertinence of it! How dared he! Did he suppose that his title gave him the right to stare at every girl as the whim prompted him? Was he so conceited that he thought she would be flattered by being noticed by him? Being ruffled and cross at the outset, Caroline became perhaps needlessly hot and bothered about the incident and not even the eager garrulity of her neighbour could take her mind off it.

Seizing a moment when the latter's attention was diverted from her in replying to a query from Mrs Digby, Caroline stole another look across the table. She felt the blood rush to her cheeks and she looked away in confusion as his cool, steady gaze met hers. But recovering quickly, she raised her eyes again and confronted him boldly across the candlelit table, her spirit now thoroughly roused, for as she had turned away before she fancied she noticed a faintly sardonic smile lurking round the corners of his lips.

For an instant they held each other in a kind of spell, oblivious of the laughter and babble of voices around them. Then he smiled, not sardonically, but pleasantly and encouragingly and his dark eyes glowed with unsuspected geniality. Caroline was dumbfounded and the colour flooded to her cheeks again; and she could scarcely believe her ears when a moment later she heard his quiet, even voice speaking to her as he leant across the table. "I have not seen your uncle for several days. He is well, I trust?"

"Oh — yes, thank you, Sir James," she answered shyly, smiling back at him.

"I hope to call on you all in a day or two," he continued. "I have had many matters to attend to lately so that I have been prevented from paying any visits."

The burglary at Court House flashed across Caroline's mind and she experienced a thrill of excitement.

"Do you think it would be convenient for me to call at the Grange tomorrow morning?" he asked.

"I think so, Sir James. My uncle has no engagements in the morning."

"Let us say tomorrow then, shall we? I shall ride over at about ten o'clock."

Caroline was unable to do more than utter a brief word of assent for Mr Lark, realising that he had lost her attention, broke into their conversation, and he gave her no further opportunity of speaking to Sir James during the rest of dinner.

Still, those few words had done much to improve her temper; and when the ladies withdrew to the drawing room at the end of dinner, she decided that she wasn't going to have the whole of her evening spoilt by being compelled to listen to Mr Lark after dinner as well. And so, on the pretext of wishing to admire the garden, she left the group of ladies round the coffee table and went and stood by one of the windows, placing herself so that she was hidden by the long, blue velvet curtain which hung down beside it.

But her ruse was a failure. Mr Lark had no intention of relinquishing the society of pretty Miss Berkley. He was foremost among the gentlemen when they came in from the dining room, and seeing that Caroline was not with the other ladies, he peered eagerly round the room, and still failing to find her, he appealed to his hostess. Caroline could have wept with vexation when she heard Mrs Digby naively reveal her hiding place. In an instant Mr Lark was beside her, all smiles and bows.

"A perfect evening, is it not?" he proclaimed, with fervour.

A curt nod was the only response he got for this rapture.

"The evening sky is superb! Such colour, such exquisite hues! A most moving spectacle, do you not think, Miss Berkley?"

"Oh, yes, I suppose so," Caroline agreed inattentively. She turned from the window. "I think I shall sit down."

She walked over to a vacant chair and Mr Lark trotted after her like a faithful dog, dragged the chair forward with needless officiousness, inquired several times at which angle she preferred it, twisted it round for her to see whether it would be better facing the fireplace or the window, and finally, when Caroline had pointed out that it would look a little odd if she sat with her back to the room, he permitted her to sit down with the chair facing exactly the way it had been before he had begun rotating it. Then, having assured himself that she felt no draught and had a clear view of the room, he went and fetched another chair and sat down beside her.

Mercifully for Caroline and fortunately for Mr Lark, Mrs Digby at that moment asked Charlotte to play for them, and as the rector bent forward to continue, with undiminished eloquence, from where he had left off he was silenced by an indignant, little frown.

After two songs Charlotte left the piano and another performer was sought. Tom Hawley proposed Harriet; but she protested that Caroline was a better player than she and therefore ought to play. Caroline denied this strenuously. But the intervention of Mr Lark, with an urgent entreaty to Miss Berkley to oblige them, settled the matter; for Tom Hawley, who did not mind which of them performed, joined everyone else in urging Caroline to play and she was forced to give in.

When she crossed the room to the piano Caroline was not a little surprised to find Sir James standing beside the instrument, arranging some music on the stand. Mr Lark, who had escorted Caroline to the piano, was also somewhat taken aback at finding the office he had intended for himself already bespoken. He hung around the piano for a minute or two while Caroline chose her music; but the baronet showed no sign of relinquishing his post and, in fact, took not the least notice of him despite the one or two tentative coughs he uttered in an attempt to draw attention to his presence, but went on quietly arranging the music for Caroline; and Mr Lark had to retire to a seat away from the piano and endure the mortification of watching Sir James turn over the music for her.

After playing two pieces, Caroline got up and left the piano. She was about to suggest that Harriet took her place but a quick glance round the room told her that her cousin was not present; nor was Tom Hawley; and smiling quietly to herself, she strolled over to the window to look out into the garden. But a second had not passed before Mr Lark was at her side again, praising her for the excellence of her performance and thanking her profusely on behalf of the whole company for having entertained them so delightfully. Caroline was by this time so weary of him that she could not trust herself to speak civilly, and she stood staring out of the window with a stony expression on her face, paying not the smallest attention to the grandiloquent encomiums being showered upon her.

"It is a tranquil scene, do you not think?"

At the sound of the quiet voice Caroline glanced up in surprise to find Sir James Reddaway standing on the other side of her.

"I beg your pardon!" he apologised, smiling down at her. "I'm afraid I startled you."

"Oh, no, of course not, Sir James!" she laughed shyly. "But I was admiring the garden and did not notice you!"

"There is a better view from the next window. Come and see."

Caroline read the meaning in the dark eyes which were fixed on her, mesmerising her as if by some strange, indefinable power; and politely begging Mr Lark to excuse her she allowed herself to be led to the third window further down the room. For once Mr Lark had the sense to realise that it would be fruitless to follow her and he went and sat down disconsolately and in something of a huff on the settee in the middle of the room.

"I thought we should never get rid of that fellow," Sir James muttered out of the side of his mouth. Then seeing the rather shocked expression which came into her face, he added "Well, you must admit you weren't exactly enjoying his company, were you?"

Caroline's cheeks went a shade pinker and she lowered her eyes, ashamed that she should have allowed her feelings to become so obvious.

"No, I wasn't!" she owned up in a small voice. She noticed the quizzical smile on his face, "How he does talk!" she exclaimed in a whisper. "He goes on and on till I feel my poor head going round in a whirl!"

He uttered a gentle chuckle. "You have, I fear, excited the admiration of the worthy rector," he observed teasingly.

"I am indeed unlucky then. But he must not think I shall be such an easy conquest," she said lightly, as if dismissing the idea as a joke.

"I am sure you would not."

There was no levity in his voice and the sudden change of tone made her glance up in surprise. There was no laughter in his eyes either and she felt suddenly afraid of him.

"But it would be exceedingly presumptuous of me to believe that Mr Lark intended to pay more attention to me than to anyone else," she said, with a nervous laugh. "It is his way to make a fuss of a lady and I don't think he means anything by it."

"Time will tell," he rejoined, a dry smile returning to his face. "By the by — I hope you will forgive me for thrusting myself upon you as I did."

"You have a perfect right to go where you please."

He bowed. "Thank you. Then may I stay here?"

"Certainly, if you wish to," she laughed coolly.

"I do wish to," came the reply.

Caroline waited tensely for him to speak again.

"I have another apology to make," he began, at length. "You must have thought me very uncivil staring at you across the table at dinner."

"I did indeed wonder why you kept looking at me, Sir James."

"I was hoping you might be prevailed upon to talk to me. You did not seem to be enjoying the society of your neighbours any more than I of mine. But you looked away so coldly at first that I feared I had offended you."

Caroline was not quite sure what to say and she felt herself blushing. "I am sorry if you have found the evening dull, sir," she said.

"I don't find it at all dull now," he returned quickly.

Caroline threw him a swift glance and turned back to the window. She wasn't sure what to make of him. Either he was amusing himself by trying to flirt with her or — whatever it was it behoved her to be careful for she did not know him very well yet. "I am relieved to know that you will not be out of temper when you leave us," she said jokingly.

"I should be sorry to think that your drive here had gone unrewarded."

"On the contrary — it has been amply rewarded. I have found a new and very charming friend."

He looked unsmilingly into her face and Caroline felt a tremor of fear run over her again.

"You are very kind, sir," she answered, with a demure inclination of her head.

While they had been talking the Digbys' daughter, Jane, had been singing, and just before she finished Harriet and Tom Hawley crept into the room through the French window. They both looked very happy and Caroline could see that her cousin was having some difficulty in preventing herself from giggling and, in fact, she nearly did disgrace herself when Tom whispered something in her ear as they sidled to a corner of the room.

When Jane had come to the end of her song Mrs Digby proposed that they should play cards and her guests gathered round her to discuss how the tables should be arranged. Caroline and Sir James took no part in the discussion, the latter because he seemed disinclined to move from the window and the former because she couldn't nerve herself to break into his meditations.

"You must think me very uncivil to daydream like this," he apologised, turning to her with a smile. "I confess I was carried away by the beauty of the evening."

"It is very peaceful," Caroline agreed.

"These tranquil, green meadows! How remote they are from all the strife and bitterness that have troubled our lives these twenty years! Oh, the futility of wars! So much is lost, so little gained!"

There was such a note of sadness in his voice that Caroline's caution deserted her temporarily and her feelings towards him softened. "Pray do not be so mournful, Sir James!" she protested gently.

"No — I don't feel mournful." he rejoined, with a smile. "Indeed, I'm exceedingly happy! This has been one of the pleasantest evenings I have ever spent! And for that I am sincerely grateful to you!" he assured her, with an earnestness that silenced her again.

In the short pause that followed she tried to summon up the courage to ask the question that she had been toying with for some little time. She glanced up at him, hesitated and then started. "Sir James — " The deep, brown eyes fixed questioningly on her and she faltered.

"Yes," he prompted when she did not continue.

"I was wondering — " before those searching eyes her courage failed her and she stopped.

"Is there something you wish to ask me?" he inquired in a gentle voice.

"No — no, it is of no consequence," she answered hastily. "'Tis not important."

He regarded her in silence for a few seconds. "I cannot believe that," he said, with the same gentleness. "The confusion and anxiety of your manner makes it evident that it is far from unimportant," he teased good-naturedly. "What is it you want to ask me?"

Caroline felt the colour rising to her face as she stood beside him with downcast eyes, knowing that he was watching her curiously, and she reproached herself for her folly.

"There isn't time to speak of it now. The others are ready and we mustn't keep them waiting," she excused herself, moving away from the window.

"Do you promise to tell me what it is later then?" he whispered as they walked over to the card tables.

Caroline nodded her head mutely and sat down, without looking at him, in the place to which she was directed by Jane. She was beginning to wish she had never thought of meddling in his affairs, and her only hope was that she might still evade giving him an answer if she could prevent herself being detached from the rest of the party again.

But it was a vain hope. For when the butler brought in the tea later in the evening Caroline found Sir James at her elbow.

"Wouldn't you rather sit on the window seat?" he suggested in an undertone. "You'd have more room than in this chair."

She was loth to agree with him, but as the others had all pushed back their chairs and risen to their feet it would have appeared odd if she had remained at the card table alone; so she rose and allowed him to lead her to the window seat.

"The pink one looks rather nice," he advised, indicating an iced cake on the plate he had brought to her with a cup of tea.

She accepted the cake without a word and waited for him to sit down beside her.

"It has been a delightful evening, don't you think?" he began, stretching his long legs out lazily.

"Yes, I have enjoyed it very much," she agreed.

He regarded her gravely. "Are you tired?"

"A little."

"You will feel better when you have had some tea. It will refresh you."

They sipped their tea in silence. Then he turned to her, and looking straight into her eyes, he said "Will you tell me what it is you want to ask me? You promised you would," he reminded her.

She lowered her eyes for a second; then lifting them to his again and taking a deep breath, she said "I hope you will not be angry with me for asking you but — is it true that Court House was broken into last night?"

She had expected him to be annoyed that his secret had been revealed, but she was not prepared for the look of intense displeasure that appeared on his face with such startling suddenness.

He stiffened visibly and his thin mouth hardened into a rigid line and a fierce, angry light glowed in his dark eyes. "How did you know? Who told you?" he demanded in rapid tones.

Caroline was too astonished to answer him at once and she felt as though she was being bewitched by those burning eyes which seemed to drive right through her. "I — one of the gardeners told me," she confessed lamely.

"Does anyone else know of it besides yourself? Have you told your family?"

"No, Sir James. I have not spoken of it to anyone. I wished to be certain of the truth of the report. That's why I asked you," she explained, with disarming frankness.

He seemed relieved by her reply and stared moodily at the floor while she watched him anxiously.

"It is true — my house was broken into last night," he acknowledged. "But I didn't wish it to be known yet lest it might cause unnecessary alarm in the district." There was a look of apology on his face as he turned to her. "I'm sorry if I seemed churlish," he said. "But I had given orders to my servants to say nothing about it as I hoped to catch the thief without having a commotion made about it. Your man will sometimes fall into a trap if he doesn't know what steps are being taken to capture him. And after all, it is really a very trivial matter," he ended, regaining his former geniality.

Caroline was conscious of a feeling of doubt about his explanation; for when she recalled his sudden wave of anger a few minutes back she found it difficult to convince herself that the matter was to be dismissed as 'trivial'. But she had no desire to provoke him any further and prudently decided to keep her thoughts to herself.

"Was anything of value stolen, Sir James?" she inquired, trying to seem sympathetic.

He shook his head. "No; that's why I decided to say nothing about it," he answered. He put his hand gently over hers. "Will you oblige me by saying nothing about it to anyone too?"

Caroline glanced nervously behind her but no one seemed to be paying any attention to them. "Of course, if you wish it!" she assured him, withdrawing her hand from his.

He leant back indolently in the corner of the window. "Thank you. I shall be infinitely obliged to you if you will help me. I know I can trust you with my secret." He smiled at her. "Perhaps I should say —

our secret for that's what it is now, isn't it?"

After that the matter was dropped; and when the time came shortly after for the guests to leave Sir James showed no sign of constraint or ill-humour when he said good night to her, and even paid her the compliment of thanking her again for having made the evening so pleasant for him; and she left Elmcross confident that she had not after all offended him seriously.

"Caroline, dearest, Tom asked me to apologise to you for having missed your songs," Harriet whispered to her, as they sat side by side in the carriage, jogging along the quiet country road to the Grange.

"I didn't mind in the least," Caroline said, smiling softly to herself. "Where did you go?"

"Into the garden to see the lily pond. Mrs Digby said we might. Oh, it was lovely!"

Whether she was referring to the lily pond or to something else, Caroline was left to guess.

"Caroline — " Harriet began again, after a pause.

"Yes?"

"Do you — like Tom?"

"Of course I do! Why?"

Another pause. "Well — because — I would like you to."

Caroline glanced sharply at the dim profile of her cousin's averted face outlined in the half-light against the carriage window.

"Harriet, have you — fallen in love with him?" she asked cautiously.

Another, much longer pause followed this question; then a small, tremulous voice answered "I don't know — yes — I think have!" Harriet turned from the window. "Oh, Caroline, what shall I do?"

Caroline put out her hand and took hold of her cousin's. "Dearest, whatever are you getting so upset about?"

"Supposing — he isn't in love with me?" Harriet gulped out tearfully.

Caroline thought rapidly for a moment. "Harriet, whose idea was it to go to look at the lily pond?"

Harriet looked at her in surprise. "Why — Tom's!" she cried. "You don't think I should have been so forward as to suggest it, do you?"

"Well, why do you think he asked you and not someone else — Charlotte Knox for instance?"

There ensued another short silence while Harriet considered this piece of logic. "Caroline, do you really think — " she whispered, clutching her cousin's hand eagerly.

"Of course, you goose! He hadn't eyes for anyone but you the whole evening! I declare it was positively uncivil of him to have ignored the rest of us so completely!" she cried gaily.

"Did he really?" Harriet murmured dreamily. "I never noticed!" She sank back into her corner with a happy, little sigh.

The two girls curled up in their corners in sleepy silence lulled by the steady clip-clop of the horses' hooves on the dry, flinty road.

"Caroline, do you like Mr Lark?"

At the sound of her cousin's gentle voice Caroline raised her drowsy head. "Not very much," she answered vaguely.

"He seemed to like you," Harriet chuckled. "He paid you a great deal of attention this evening, I noticed."

The memory of her wearisome experiences earlier in the evening brought a tiny scowl to Caroline's face. "I couldn't help that!" she retorted peevishly.

"Didn't you like it?" her cousin queried innocently.

"No, I didn't!" came the response grumpily.

"Then you don't like him at all?" pursued Harriet.

"No, I do not! He pestered me the whole evening with his silly compliments till I was nearly demented and I shan't mind if I never see him again!"

"Not the whole evening," Harriet corrected softly.

Caroline was on the point of demanding what she meant when her own memory enlightened her. She became suddenly on the defensive and turned her face to the window.

"Sir James Reddaway seemed to be paying you quite a lot of attention too," Harriet said.

"Oh, only for a little while," Caroline replied modestly.

"It seemed more than a little while to me — most of the evening," Harriet maintained. "Was he nice?"

"Yes — quite."

"What did you talk about?" Harriet pressed curiously, in no way damped by her cousin's reticence.

"Oh — various things — the garden and the weather and things like that."

"Is that all?" Harriet was now a little disappointed and at the same time not much convinced. "Didn't he talk about himself at all?"

Caroline's head swung round abruptly. "What did Tom talk to you about when you went to the lily pond?" she demanded in an aggressive manner.

A high-pitched giggle floated up from the opposite corner of the carriage. "I'm sorry, Caroline! It was naughty of me to have been so inquisitive!" Harriet chortled. "But I'm so glad Sir James likes you. I shouldn't care for you to marry Mr Lark."

Caroline stared at her in frigid silence for several seconds. "*What*!"

"Surely you must have guessed that's the reason why he's so attentive to you."

Caroline was too appalled to speak. "Oh — it's like his impudence!" she burst out wrathfully at last. "How dare he contemplate such a thing!" This final affront released the tide of irritation that had accumulated against the Rector of Cullaton. "Well, he'll soon find out he's much mistaken if he thinks he's going to make me fall in love with him!" she declared furiously.

She sat bolt upright, her hands clenched in her lap and her eyes flashing angrily, quivering with indignation and, it is to be regretted, through bad temper.

"There now, don't get so cross about it!" Harriet expostulated soothingly. "He'll find out he's wrong eventually and then you'll never be bothered by him again."

"But he's so dreadfully dense that it will take ages to convince him!" her cousin wailed.

"No, it won't, I'm sure," Harriet argued confidently. "And if Mrs Knox or anyone else encourages him and tries to make you marry him Tom and I will stand up for you. Tom can't abide him! He says he'd like to see him ducked in the village pond!" she ended, with a malicious, little chuckle.

Caroline sank back in her corner, too weary to argue about it any more, and neither of them spoke again till they got home. And after they had given Mr and Mrs Allen a brief description of the party they went upstairs to bed.

Alone in her room, Caroline was in a pensive mood as she began to undress. The conversation in the carriage had riled her not a little. It was easy for Harriet to treat the matter light-heartedly; Mr Lark wasn't Tom Hawley, nor even remotely like him. It wasn't going to be so simple to shake Mr Lark off, she felt sure. Presumably, because she was an orphan, he thought she would have a less independent mind and would accept the first offer of marriage she got. Oh, how maddening it all was! She slammed her hairbrush viciously down on the dressing table and began pacing up and down the room. Conceited idiot! How she detested his ridiculous bowing and smirking and his silly, insincere flatteries! She flung herself on her back on the bed and lay staring moodily up at the canopy. And what right had Mrs Knox to interfere in her affairs, she demanded angrily, seeing that lady's insinuations in a new light? It was no concern of hers whom she married or even whether she got married at all. Mrs Knox was always trying to manage other people's affairs for them. Well, she wasn't going to manage hers, Caroline decided firmly. She could be as nasty as she liked but she shouldn't have her own way this time. Poor Mrs Digby! How distressed she would have been had she known what a deplorable effect her dinner party had had upon her young guest.

Having relieved her feelings a little, Caroline got up and walked thoughtfully over to the dressing table. What a strange man Sir James Reddaway was, she reflected, as she straightened one of the tall candles! He looked so reserved and unfriendly, yet when one got to know him he was really rather nice. A dreamy smile entered her face and she sat with her elbows resting on the dressing table, lost in thought. Then, abruptly, the smile left her face. But was he so charming? Was there another side to his character that she had not seen, she wondered? It was obvious that he hadn't liked her asking about the burglary at his house and his sudden change of manner had quite frightened her. But why should he have been so angry? He had declared it to be only a trivial matter, excused himself for not having told anyone about it on that account, and yet she felt quite certain he was much put out about it. Could it be that he was annoyed that his servants had disregarded his orders? A feeling of compunction came over her at the thought of getting some unlucky groom into trouble. But no, she felt there was some deeper mystery behind it all. Her fingers toyed idly with some trinkets lying on the dressing table as she tried to discover a solution to these puzzling circumstances. Then all at once she looked up, her eyes bright with enlightenment, her mouth formed in the shape of an unspoken 'oh', as a new and startling possibility occurred to her. Perhaps ... perhaps Sir James himself was the Midnight Horseman!

Inspired by this intriguing surmise, Caroline got up, and going over to the open window, she drew back the curtains and leant out over the stone sill. It was dark now and below her the flagged paths gleamed whitely in the light of the moon against the dark shapes of the box hedges. Ahead of her a solitary light shone in a cottage window, a lonely amber glow winking feebly out of the surrounding darkness. The tiniest sounds were magnified by the eerie stillness of the night; the tinkling ripple of the brook just beyond the garden wall and the hushed rustle of the breeze whispering through the trees; and in the distance the sharp, strident note of a dog's bark from some remote farmstead echoed intermittently across the silent fields.

Caroline remained at the window, lost in thought, for several minutes. Then she turned her head slowly round to the right where she could discern the dark mass of Cullaton Moor. How dismal and frightening it looked up there, she thought! No friendly light winked at her out of the darkness, no dog barked to remind her of the existence of living creatures. It was dead, dead as the wretched felon they had hanged there half a century ago, a bleak, desolate stretch of moorland.

And as she peered into the darkness Caroline couldn't help wondering if, even at that very moment, the mysterious horseman was riding up the lonely moorland road to Cullaton Cross, and a tiny thrill raced through her body as she conjectured as to whether it might be the man to whom she had been talking only a short while ago in the cheerful drawing room at Elmcross. Certainly they knew very little about Sir James. He rarely stayed at Court House for more than a few weeks at a time and when he was there he did not mix very freely. But what could be his reason for masquerading in the guise of a legendary highwayman, if he it was? Had he some nefarious purpose for riding on the moor at night? Was he a smuggler? She shook her head. That seemed hardly likely so far inland A highwayman? But again she decided that this could not be the answer; there were few travellers on the moor for him to rob. Was he a madman? The memory of those strange, burning eyes came into her mind and she shuddered involuntarily and withdrew from the window. It surely couldn't be that he was some maniac who was obsessed with a passion for that lonely moor or who imagined himself as the ghost of the dead highwayman. Caroline drew the curtains together and returned to the dressing table in a sombre mood.

But it would be fun to see the Midnight Horseman, she said to herself again in a minute or two as she went on with her undressing. And it would show people that she wasn't the sort of girl who was going to let herself be shut up in a frowsty old parsonage all her life. Mrs Lark indeed! The very thought revolted her! She flung her clothes down on the floor around her in a sudden burst of ill-temper, not caring what the housemaid would think when she saw the disordered state of the room in the morning. It was her room and they were her petticoats and pantalettes and she'd do what she liked with them!

In this heated and mutinous frame of mind she climbed into bed and snuffed the candle. Dare she go out on to Cullaton Moor after dark? She longed to find out more about the mysterious stranger who rode about up there when everyone else was at home in snug, warm beds. She nestled cosily under the bedclothes, all kinds of romantic fancies running through her head, and in a few minutes was fast asleep.

Chapter Five

"What was Charlotte Knox wearing last night?" Mrs Allen inquired of her daughter, as the three ladies of the Grange sat in the drawing room after breakfast the next morning.

"Oh — a light blue dress," Harriet informed her vaguely.

"Did she look well in it?" pursued her mother, by no means satisfied with this meagre description.

"Oh, yes, Mama, she looked charming! I'm sure she was quite the handsomest girl in the room!"

"I don't see why she should have been!" her mother objected. "You are quite as handsome as Charlotte — both of you," she added, glancing across at her niece who was sitting by the window, her head bent over her needlework. "You should not be so quick to underrate yourselves. Only last Sunday old Mr Hawley confided in me as we were coming out of church that he thought you were two of the handsomest girls he knew."

"I am sure that is not quite true," Harriet declared, with a bashful laugh. "Mr Hawley always liked us better than most other girls and I think he is inclined to be prejudiced in our favour."

"Of course he is not!" Mrs Allen contradicted sharply. "Mr Hawley is not one to give praise where it is not merited. He is most discriminating and you should be proud of having made such a good impression on him."

"I'm very glad he likes us," Harriet said, conscious of a glow of pleasure in her heart.

"Whom did you sit beside at dinner?" was her mother's next question.

Harriet hesitated an instant and a faint flush coloured her cheeks. "Tom Hawley," she answered in a low voice.

"And did you find him a pleasant companion?"

"Oh, yes," Harriet agreed airily.

"I am pleased to hear that. I think you make a very suitable pair for you are alike in temperament and outlook. Do you not think so?"

"I — er — yes, we may have a little in common," Harriet admitted cautiously.

"There can be no doubt of that. And I am quite certain that Tom Hawley admires you a great deal, my dear." Mrs Allen paused a moment to observe the effect this had upon her daughter; but Harriet was not to be drawn and kept her head bent low over her sewing. "How would you like Tom Hawley for a husband?" her mother proposed, unable to contain her patience any longer.

Harriet's blue eyes looked up at her in consternation and her cheeks glowed scarlet with embarrassment. "Oh, Mama, how can you ask such a question!"

"You need not be so put out about it," Mrs Allen retorted calmly. "I merely wished to know whether you could like him enough to marry him. I should not be at all surprised if he was to make you an offer and then you would have to make your mind up."

Harriet was feeling very indignant with her mother for discussing such a delicate matter in front of her cousin. "It's — well — I don't know him sufficiently well," she said somewhat incoherently.

"Very well, we will say no more about it now," her mother said graciously, not dissatisfied with the result of her inquiries which showed that there were possibilities to be hoped for. "Whom did Charlotte sit next to?" she asked, reverting to the Elmcross party.

"Sir James Reddaway, I think. It was Sir James, was it not, Caroline?" Harriet said, appealing to her cousin.

"Yes."

The sound of her quiet voice reminded her aunt of her presence. "Who took you in to dinner, Caroline?" she asked.

"Mr Lark."

"And did you find him a pleasant companion?" Mrs Allen inquired for the second time in five minutes.

"Quite."

"Was he attentive to you?"

"He was very polite."

"Yes, I should have expected that," Mrs Allen said tartly, not much pleased with this indefinite answer. "One would not have supposed that he would have been anything less. What I meant was — did he pay you particular attention during the evening?"

"I don't think so."

"Did he offer to turn the music for you when you played?"

"No."

"He did not! That is surprising! Did you have no one to turn the

40

music for you?"

"Oh, yes. Sir James Reddaway was kind enough to do it for me," Caroline informed her, with a certain inward glee.

Mrs Allen's astonishment was evident. She started perceptibly and stared at Caroline as if she doubted whether she had heard her aright. "Sir James!"

"He was waiting by the piano when Caroline went to it," Harriet broke in impetuously. "Mr Lark would have liked to have turned the music for her but Sir James had got there first!"

"There is no need to speak of it like that, Harriet! It sounds most undignified!" her mother rebuked, with a frown. "Presumably Sir James happened to be standing near to the piano when Caroline went to play and naturally he offered to turn the music for her since it would have been accounted uncivil of him if he had not."

Harriet doubted very much it was mere chance that brought Sir James in the vicinity of the piano when Caroline came to play; but she was not disposed to argue the point with her mother and contented herself with saying "Mr Lark looked most disappointed and I'm sure he was exceedingly envious of Sir James."

"Maybe he was," Mrs Allen said, dismissing the incident hurriedly. "You haven't forgotten you are driving over to Cullaton with Miss Merrilock tomorrow, have you, Caroline?"

"No, Aunt Julia."

"I expect you will visit the Rectory while you are there. Miss Merrilock will undoubtedly wish to see her old home again and I understand Mr Lark has promised to be in to receive you."

Fortunately Mrs Allen was so taken up with what she was saying that she did not observe her niece's face. If she had she would have been shocked to see the pretty, red mouth twist in a grimace of disgust.

"That's very kind of him," Caroline remarked in a flat voice.

"Yes, it is," Mrs. Allen affirmed promptly. "And you realise to whom the compliment is being paid, don't you?"

No immediate reply was forthcoming to this awkward question and Mrs Allen glanced sharply at her niece.

"Yes ... I suppose so," the later admitted grudgingly.

"Suppose! Suppose, indeed! You're being uncommonly modest! Of course that's why he has promised to be in to receive you and Miss Merrilock!" Mrs Allen was finding her niece's unresponsive attitude most exasperating and she was inclined to get up and go and shake her into some sort of animation. "Well, are you pleased?" she demanded impatiently.

"Yes," came the brief, monosyllabic reply, drawled out with such an entire absence of emotion that Mrs Allen could not but remain unconvinced.

"You don't appear to be," she said, not at all content with the way things were going. "You don't usually suppress your feelings like this, Caroline. You like Mr Lark, don't you?"

Caroline's eyes fluttered upwards and she appeared to take a deep breath. If only old Dr Merrilock hadn't gone out in the snow last December and caught cold!

"Caroline! I am speaking to you!"

Her aunt's voice brought Caroline out of her gloomy ponderings. "Oh, yes, he's very agreeable," she answered dully.

"Agreeable is that all you can say for him?" her aunt exclaimed testily.

"I don't know him well enough to say more than that."

"You have known him long enough to form an opinion of him. You have met him several times now at houses in the neighbourhood and you have heard him take the service when the archdeacon was away. You cannot deny that you have had ample opportunity of discovering what sort of a person he is." Mrs Allen paused in the hope that this might stir her niece into saying something. But Caroline did not even look at her, continuing to sew, a sullen expression on her face. "Tell me — do you not think he is a charming man?"

"He may be."

If her niece had not been so far away Mrs Allen would probably have got up and given her a good shaking and, indeed, might so far have forgotten herself as to have administered a sharp slap, so infuriated was she becoming at the girl's indifference. "May be! May be!" she repeated heatedly. "Why, Caroline, are you completely blind? Have you not perceived that Mr Lark is in love with you?"

Her aunt's meaning was now quite clear and Caroline realised that she was on the brink of a desperate conflict. "No, I had no idea," she replied, turning to her aunt and trying to appear surprised.

Mrs Allen gaped at her incredulously. "Well, I am astounded! Utterly astounded!" she exclaimed. "Well, you may as well know now, Caroline, that Mr Lark intends to make you an offer."

"Does he?"

Mrs Allen threw up her hands in extreme irritation and flung round on her angrily. "Can you not show more feeling, child! I might be speaking to you of the weather the little interest you display! Can you not understand that this is a matter of the greatest importance to you?"

"Oh, yes, Aunt Julia, I do understand that."

"Then be good enough to show more interest in what I am saying. Now — how do you like the idea of marrying Mr Lark?"

The crisis had been reached, and Caroline nerved herself to deliver the answer which she knew would raise one of the greatest storms the Grange had ever experienced and place her under a cloud for weeks to come.

"I don't," she said flatly.

"*Caroline!*"

Mrs Allen's scandalised voice rang through the room, making Harriet, who had been listening to the conversation with growing uneasiness, look up with a horrified expression and her eyes darted fearfully between the faces of her mother and her cousin.

Caroline was on her feet now, facing her aunt boldly, a determined look in her eyes. "Aunt Julia, it isn't any use my pretending to you that I should like to marry Mr Lark. I don't admire him and I doubt if I ever shall and I should rather remain single all my life than marry a man I didn't love!"

"And I suppose you expect your uncle to go on providing for you for the rest of your life!"

"No, I should try to earn my own living."

"Oh, you're a foolish girl!" Mrs Allen cried. "I really have no patience with you! Here are your uncle and I trying to do our best for you, yet you will not stop to listen for one instant to our advice! I consider your attitude most reprehensible, Caroline, most reprehensible!"

Caroline reflected upon this; then she asked "Does Uncle George think I should marry Mr Lark?" There was just the faintest note of anxiety in her voice as she spoke.

"I — well — I haven't mentioned it to him yet," her aunt admitted. "But I have no doubt he will agree with me when I put the matter to him," she concluded confidently.

There was a little smile of triumph in Caroline's face as she turned away. She knew she could depend upon her uncle if he realised she was being unjustly treated.

"Your uncle knows as well as I do how difficult it is to find suitable husbands," Mrs Allen began again. "He will not wish such a good chance to be wasted any more than I."

As Caroline did not seem inclined to speak and Mrs Allen's eloquence was temporarily exhausted there was an uncomfortable silence; and Harriet, who could not bear a silence at any time, least of all when it was charged with tension as it was then, looked up and said "Mama, would it not be best to wait and see if Mr Lark does make Caroline an offer? He may change his mind yet."

If she had hoped to calm the troubled waters with this ingenuous suggestion she was quickly undeceived by her mother. "Mind your own business, Harriet!" she commanded crushingly. "This has nothing to do with you! There is not the slightest possibility of Mr Lark changing his mind! He has already shown his intentions beyond a doubt and it would be unpardonable if he was to withdraw now!"

"Yes, Mama, but I thought — "

"Never mind what you thought!" Mrs Allen interrupted curtly. "I do not wish to know your opinion. I merely wished to ascertain Caroline's feelings and I must say I am sorry to find her so headstrong and so unmindful of her duty to your father and myself. But if she is so determined to disregard our advice she will have only herself to blame if she dies an old maid. At least we shall have done our duty towards her," she ended, with a grim emphasis on the word 'duty'.

Seeing the full force of her aunt's wrath thus directed on the luckless Harriet who was cowering on the settee almost in tears, Caroline felt impelled to go to her rescue. "Please don't think me ungrateful, Aunt Julia," she said in a conciliatory tone. "I should be sorry if you thought me wanting in gratitude after all you and Uncle George have done for me."

"But you are wanting in gratitude!" Mrs Allen challenged shrilly. "Your rejection of my advice is the mark of the highest ingratitude! Here you have an opportunity of being settled in a secure and comfortable home of your own and you dismiss it without a moment's consideration!"

"I'm sorry, Aunt Julia. Perhaps I have been a little hasty," Caroline confessed. "But as I don't think I am ever likely to feel any strong affection for Mr Lark I thought it best to tell you at once lest you might receive a false impression of my regard for him."

Mrs Allen's mood changed quickly and handled tactfully she was easily mollified. And now that Caroline seemed to be adopting a less intransigent attitude she was prepared to say nothing more for the time being in the hope that perseverance on Mr Lark's part and a little sober reflection on Caroline's might ultimately bring about the satisfactory conclusion she desired. She was annoyed with herself for having introduced her husband's name into the conversation. He hadn't a high opinion of the young man, she remembered, and so far from helping to persuade Caroline to give in he might well support the recalcitrant girl and that would be exceedingly tiresome. Therefore Mrs Allen decided that it would be wisest to let the matter drop for the present. "Well, I hope you are going to be sensible, my dear," she said. "It will be a great pity indeed if such a splendid chance is missed. I am sure no one is more anxious than I that you should be happily married."

The discussion was brought to an end at this point by the entry of the very person they had been talking about. As the silvery chimes of the clock on the mantelpiece tinkled out eleven o'clock Mr Allen came into the drawing room with Mr Lark.

"Julia, my dear, Mr Lark has come over from Cullaton to pay us a visit," Mr Allen said, with an absence of enthusiasm that suggested that he was sorry he happened to be at home that morning.

"I had business with the archdeacon in Emberhope and so I thought I would seize the opportunity of calling on my good friends at the Grange," Mr Lark explained as he shook hands with Mrs Allen.

"We are delighted to see you, Mr Lark," she responded cordially. "It is very good of you to call especially when you must be so busy just now in your new parish."

"Oh, but never too busy to be unable to find the time to participate in the diversions and relaxations of cultivated society, ma'am," he assured her, with a deprecatory wave of his hand. "As I was saying to the archdeacon only this morning, the refinements of higher society must not be neglected by those of us who are called upon to minister to the ignorant and unsophisticated people of our countryside."

"Undoubtedly, undoubtedly!" interposed Mr Allen who was listening with an air of mild surprise.

"Er — yes — quite — as you say, sir," the rector stuttered, momentarily put out of his stride. "And good-hearted as my simple parishioners are," he commenced again, "their homely, rustic ways have their limitations and it is therefore necessary for those of us who labour among them to seek more rational and informed intercourse within the circle of such as are our equals in intellect and erudition. As I was saying to the archdeacon —"

Mr Allen did not intend having his morning wasted by being compelled to hear all that Mr Lark had said to the archdeacon, of which there seemed no end. "Will you not sit down, sir?" he interrupted, pushing forward a chair.

"Thank you, sir. As I was saying," the young man recommenced, sitting down in the centre of the room. "I told the archdeacon that I considered Ullingham Grange quite one of the most delightful houses to visit in the whole of Northumberland, not only on account of its antiquity and the pleasantness of its situation, but also for the truly refreshing and elevating society of its inmates. The archdeacon was in complete agreement with me and was kind enough to express the opinion that we were most fortunate in having such an amiable and accomplished family in our midst." He leant back in his chair, a self-satisfied simper on his lips, awaiting with confidence the delighted reactions of his listeners.

"We are grateful to the archdeacon for his kind testimonial," Mr Allen said gravely, though the tiny wrinkles at the corners of his eyes betrayed his true feelings. "We shall do our best to provide you with that refined and enlightened society to which you are accustomed, sir. I trust our conversation may always be suitably edifying and will afford you the recreation you seek to compensate you for your labours among your parishioners."

"Indeed I do, sir! Most edifying!" Mr Lark assured him earnestly. "There is nothing I enjoy more than a quiet half-hour in convivial intercourse with my friends. Though I make no claim to be a brilliant conversationalist I fancy I can contribute my fair share to a discussion no matter the subject."

"You are to be congratulated on your versatility, sir," Mr Allen commented drily.

"Oh, it is nothing, sir! It is but a gift with which I have had the good fortune to be endowed just as your charming daughter has been endowed with that grace and vivacity that make her such a valued asset to our society." Mr Lark beamed benignly on Harriet. "And I would add — your equally, charming niece," he said, turning to the window. "Oh — she is not here!" he exclaimed, the gallant smile being replaced by a look of surprise.

That was perfectly true. When Mr Lark had come into the drawing room Caroline had been sitting at a window. But having no wish to draw attention to herself, she had retreated surreptitiously to a settee at the far end of the room where she was working with her head bent over her sewing, apparently paying not the smallest attention to the conversation.

"Caroline is at the other end of the room," Mr Allen pointed out. "Since she seems to be engrossed in her work allow me to thank you on her behalf for your compliments." He looked across at his niece with a smile. "Caroline, my dear, what is it you are doing?"

Caroline raised her head and smiled at him. "I'm embroidering my initials on this handkerchief, Uncle George," she told him, holding up a flimsy square of lawn.

By doing so she gave Mr Lark the opportunity he had been waiting for, and he jumped up from his chair with an eager light in his eyes. "May I see it?" he begged, bowing before her.

Caroline held the handkerchief up for his inspection, at the same time keeping her head turned away from him.

"How exquisitely they are done! Such delicate workmanship! Quite perfect! Quite perfect!" he cooed, in a rapture, touching the edge of the handkerchief as though it was some fragile ornament. "Your niece is an excellent needlewoman, ma'am," he was kind enough to inform Mrs Allen.

"Yes, Caroline and Harriet are both proficient at that kind of sewing," she said. "They had the benefit of learning from an excellent governess

I engaged for them. I have always believed that girls should be taught to sew well for it is of value even if it is only as a pastime."

"I am entirely of your opinion, ma'am," Mr Lark said, making the few yards of carpet in front of Caroline his platform. "It is most important — indeed, I would say essential — that we should each of us have some suitable occupation in which to engage our leisure time. It is for want of a commendable way of employing their leisure that so many of our fellow citizens in the world today are tempted into degrading and corrupting dissipations. Recreation, besides affording pleasure, should refresh the body and improve the mind."

While he had been speaking Bertram, Mr Allen's butler, had entered the room. He coughed discreetly to attract attention and Mr Lark was compelled to give way before him. "Sir James Reddaway has called, ma'am."

"Sir James Reddaway!" Mrs Allen exclaimed. "Oh — well, ask him to come in, Bertram!"

Bertram walked unhurriedly into the hall and returned a moment later to announce the new caller. Mr Lark, meanwhile, had seated himself beside Caroline on the settee.

"I am on my way to Hexham," Sir James said, when he had shaken hands with Mr and Mrs Allen. "So I thought I would call in and see if there are any commissions I can undertake for any of you," he went on, speaking in a precise, businesslike tone.

"That is very obliging of you, Sir James," Mrs Allen replied. "But shall we not be putting you to a great deal of trouble?"

"None at all! I shall be delighted to be of service to you!"

"Well, I am sure it is very good of you," Mrs Allen said. "I don't think there is anything I require; but what about you, Harriet?" she asked.

But since Harriet had spent most of her quarter's allowance on a shopping expedition a week ago she, too, was unable to avail herself of the offer.

"Perhaps your niece has some commission for me," Sir James ventured, with a smiling glance in Caroline's direction.

"Oh, no, there's no need for you to trouble yourself, Sir James!" Mrs Allen intervened in her managing way. "Caroline will not be requiring anything!"

Sir James looked at Caroline and raised his eyebrows questioningly. But she could not very well contradict her aunt and shook her head with a demure, little smile.

"Are you staying the night there, Sir James?" Mr Allen inquired.

"No, Sir. I hope to get my business done in time for me to ride back again before sunset. As it's such a fine day I thought I'd take the opportunity of exercising a new horse I have bought," he explained, strolling over to the window.

"I hope you will not be detained on your journey in any way, Sir James," Mrs Allen remarked anxiously. "I should not like to think of you crossing Cullaton Moor after nightfall."

"I think I shall manage to be home before then," he said, with a smile. "And even if I'm not, I wager I can take care of myself on the moor."

"But you never know whom you may meet there," Mrs Allen persisted. "There are some very bad characters about the roads at night."

"I think you are a little hard on our beautiful moor," Sir James laughed. "I don't think it merits such an evil reputation as that."

"But it does, Sir James!" chimed in Mr Lark, impatient to join in the conversation. "Haven't you heard of the mysterious horseman who has been seen riding the moor at night?"

Sir James regarded him coldly. "I have heard of him — yes."

"Then don't you think you would be taking a great risk if you were to cross the moor after dark? I mean — you might meet this man," the rector pointed out.

"Possibly — if there is such a person."

The baronet's sceptical tone made them all turn and look at him in astonishment.

"But do you doubt it, Sir James?" queried Mrs Allen.

He walked slowly towards the centre of the room. "Indeed I do, ma'am. I regard this ridiculous superstition of the phantom horseman as utter nonsense."

This was too much for Harriet who saw all her thrilling fancies swept away if Sir James's views were allowed to prevail. "Oh, but 'tis not, Sir James!" she protested almost indignantly. "Lots of people have seen the Midnight Horseman, so it can't be just imagination!"

"Yes, yes, I agree with Miss Allen entirely!" Mr Lark seconded, with energy. "I think you are a little unjust to our good folk, sir. Old Jonathan Blackman, the sexton at Cullaton, has seen the Midnight Horseman himself and I know he would not invent a falsehood for I can assure you he is a man of the highest probity."

"No doubt — when he's sober," commented the baronet coolly.

Mr Lark jerked forward as if somebody had stuck a pin into him. "My dear sir! How can you suggest such a thing!" he cried, throwing up his hands in horrified protest. "Old Blackman is a most respectable man and in no way addicted to liquor! Indeed, I do not think there is any man in my parish whom I would rather hold up as an example of temperance and frugality than him!"

A derisive smile crossed the baronet's face and he turned away, evidently not a little diverted by the rector's gullibility. "Nevertheless, sir, it will take more than the fanciful accounts of a handful of credulous yokels to convince me!" he retorted uncompromisingly.

"Well, whether he's a ghost or not something ought to be done about him," Mrs Allen stated emphatically. She turned to her husband "George, what are you going to do about it?"

Mr Allen, who had been listening to the exchange between the other two gentlemen with no little enjoyment, was taken unawares by this question. "Me, my dear! I — well, what would you have me do?" he stammered, in some confusion.

"You must take steps to have the man apprehended so that you can find out what he is up to. It is your duty as a justice. Surely you realise that?"

Mr Allen was tempted to point out that his duties as a magistrate required him to try offenders and no more; but he was unwilling to provoke his wife in front of his visitors and he took the safer course of agreeing with her. "I will do what I can, my dear, but it's a little difficult at present because we are not sure —."

"It isn't difficult at all!" his wife interrupted him brusquely. "You must go and search for him!"

Mr Allen stared at her, aghast. "What — all alone!" he gasped.

"How stupid you are, George!" Mrs Allen exclaimed crossly, unmindful of the presence of the others. "Of course I don't mean you to go alone! You must take some of the men from the town with you!"

Mr Allen rubbed his cheek thoughtfully while he considered this proposal. "I doubt whether it would be very easy to find volunteers for such an enterprise," he demurred. "And I think I'm a bit too old for that sort of thing now."

"Then I suppose you'd rather us all to be murdered in our beds?" Mrs Allen accused in tragic tones.

"My dear — no! Pray do not get so agitated! There can be surely no fear of anything so dreadful as that happening!"

Things might have gone badly for Mr Allen had he not been rescued by the vanity of Mr Lark who, perceiving an opportunity of exciting the admiration of the ladies, entered the discussion. "Do not alarm yourself, ma'am," he began, rising to his feet though without moving far from the settee. "I shall endeavour to apprehend the man myself. I have a plan which I intend to put into instant action and I feel confident that it will be attended with success."

Sir James, who had been standing by the window, turned round with an air of interest on hearing this.

"I am glad to hear that, Mr Lark," Mrs Allen said. "I know I shall not sleep a wink at night until he is caught."

"What is it you intend to do, Mr Lark?"

Delighted to be afforded a chance of submitting his plan, the rector beamed good-humouredly on Sir James Reddaway from whom the inquiry had come. "I shall collect a party of men from my parish and lead them on to the moor where we shall lie in wait for the man. Then when he appears we shall surround him and take him prisoner." He scanned Sir James's face with eager confidence as he waited for him to pronounce judgment.

"And just where do you intend to lay this ambush? The moor is a large place, you know," the latter observed.

"There is that problem," Mr Lark acknowledged. "But as the Midnight Horseman has usually been seen near the crossroads I shall post my men there," he explained cheerfully.

"By which time your quarry will be several miles away."

The sunny smile faded slowly from the young clergyman's face and he gazed bleakly at the baronet. "Oh! Why, sir?"

"Because your ardent followers will have made enough noise to wake up their forefathers in Cullaton churchyard," he was informed, with barely concealed sarcasm.

"Oh, certainly not, Sir James!" he objected, much piqued at having his magnificent plan treated with such scant respect. "I shall warn them particularly before we set out that they must move with the utmost stealth and in complete silence."

"Then you are very sanguine, sir, if you believe that your orders will be obeyed." Sir James uttered a laugh that was almost scornful. "Why — it will be impossible for them to keep silent! They'll be grunting and cursing the whole way as well as falling into ditches and dropping their arms — I presume you'll arm them — till you'd wished you'd never brought them."

For once Mr Lark had nothing to say, and he stood in glum silence while everyone waited for him to suggest an alternative plan; but none was forthcoming. "Well, what do you suggest I do instead?" he blustered, conscious that he was cutting a poor figure.

A sly smile hovered over the baronet's face as he returned to the window. "Go yourself — but alone."

This proposal did not seem to appeal to the rector at all and he became more uncomfortable still. "Oh — well — I don't think that would be much good," he argued.

"No, nor do I," rejoined Sir James promptly. "But there'd be more sense in that than parading an army of louts on the moor."

Mr Lark was beginning to be heartily sorry that he had ever been so rash as to mention any plan, for, as he feverishly racked his brain for a way out of his embarrassment, he realised that he had committed himself to doing something about capturing the Midnight Horseman; and that, he felt, wasn't going to be so easy. "Well — I'll consider your suggestion," he muttered doubtfully, "and perhaps I might try it if — "

"You can summon up enough courage?" prompted Sir James, with a mischievous twinkle.

"Oh, no, of course not, sir!" Mr Lark expostulated indignantly. "There can be no question of that! But obviously the more men we have the less chance there is of him escaping," he argued in an attempt to retrieve his position.

"Yes, he is an elusive fellow — if he exists at all," Sir James remarked quietly, turning to the window again. "But never mind the Midnight Horseman, my friend," he continued affably. "Come and look at the moor from this window. It's a sight well worth seeing on a day like this."

His invitation was accepted promptly for Mr Lark was only too glad to change the subject after his clumsy attempt to win the admiration of the ladies had ended so dismally. So assembling as much dignity as he could, he strolled over to the window. "Ah, yes, it is indeed a splendid sight!" he agreed effusively. "Magnificent! Magnificent! You are fortunate in having such an uninterrupted view, sir," he observed condescendingly to Mr Allen.

"Yes, we are," agreed the latter, joining them at the window.

Caroline was paying no attention to the gentlemen; at least, not visually. Now why, she wondered, had Sir James been so reluctant to believe in the Midnight Horseman? So far as she knew he was the only person who had questioned the truth of the reports, which, after all, had been substantiated by several different people. And why had he been so scornful of Mr Lark's plan to catch the horseman? It was almost as if he had not wanted it to be put into action, as if he had been trying to dissuade Mr Lark, or anyone else for that matter, from searching for the Midnight Horseman. Even if he didn't place much faith in the word of the villagers who claimed to have seen the man, he surely could have no reason for opposing a plan which might prove whether he actually existed. Or could he? It was all very mystifying. Sir James's strange behaviour when she had asked him about the burglary at his house came to her mind. Dare she believe that he was the Midnight Horseman? No, it seemed impossible!. Yet — it was difficult to understand his rather suspicious behaviour. Caroline became so deeply absorbed in these interesting speculations that she failed to notice that someone was standing just behind her.

"May I sit down for a moment?"

She uttered a tiny gasp and looked up in confusion to find the person who had been the centre of her thoughts bending over her. "Oh — yes, of course, Sir James!" she stammered, moving up the settee and averting her scarlet face hastily.

"I must be off shortly," he said, sitting down beside her. "Now are you certain there's nothing I can get you in Hexham? I wished to ask you myself because I felt you were influenced by your aunt when you refused before."

He gave her such a warm and friendly smile that she felt there could be no harm in changing her mind. There was something she wanted, and as it was unlikely that she would be going to Hexham for several weeks it seemed a pity to lose this chance of getting her purchase made for her. "I wonder — do you think you could get me *The House on the Bridge*? The bookseller hadn't a copy when we were there last week."

"Nothing will give me greater pleasure," he replied. "I want to pay a visit to the bookshop myself. You shall have it tomorrow."

He was prevented from saying any more by the return of Mr Lark who, having suddenly noticed that Sir James was no longer standing beside him, had turned to perceive, not without a pang of jealousy, the whispering couple on the settee. He moved stiffly into the centre of the room where he fidgeted about, casting reproachful, sidelong glances in the direction of the settee till his presence was noticed.

"I beg your pardon, sir," Sir James apologised, getting up. "I have taken your seat."

"Pray do not disturb yourself on my account, Sir James!" Mr Lark replied in a slightly offended tone.

"Oh, I'm not doing that," the baronet rejoined curtly, walking past him. "If you will excuse me, ma'am, I must be on my way," he said to Mrs Allen.

With his departure the little gathering broke up; and shortly after the girls heaved thankful sighs as they watched Mr Lark trotting down the drive on his cob.

Chapter Six

"Caroline, do you like Sir James Reddaway?"

The two girls were alone in the old nursery that afternoon. In a distant wing of the house, the nursery had come to be regarded as their own private sanctum where they were free to air grievances, exchange confidences and behave as they liked for they had few visitors there; even Mrs Allen rarely intruded upon them, and when she did she would merely put her head round the door and comment critically on the untidiness of the room.

"Yes, of course I like him," Caroline answered, without looking up from the book she was reading.

"I'm so glad," Harriet murmured, lying back in a rickety chair, a dreamy smile on her face.

Something in the tone of her cousin's voice made Caroline look up and stare at her anxiously. "Harriet — you don't mean — Harriet, have you fallen in love with him!" she queried gropingly.

The dreamy smile faded from Harriet's face. "Oh, no, Caroline! What would be the use when he's already in love with you?" she cried.

The book in Caroline's lap fell to the floor with a thud as she sprang off the window seat. "In love with me! Harriet, what do you mean?"

"You aren't going to pretend you didn't know that, are you?" Harriet challenged.

"I'm not pretending anything!" Caroline denied hotly. "Why — it's nonsense! Sir James couldn't possibly be in love with me!"

"I'm certain he is," Harriet maintained confidently.

Caroline contemplated her with a puzzled frown. "Whatever makes you think he is?" she said.

"Because he pays you so much attention."

"He doesn't pay me any more attention than anyone else."

"Yes, he does," Harriet countered. "Haven't you noticed how he always contrives to sit beside you? Why, nobody else matters when

53

you're about! I know he's in love with you!"

"Of course he isn't!"

But Harriet was not to be put off. "Didn't you see how he purposely chose to sit by you when he called this morning?" she argued doggedly.

"Oh, how stupid you are, Harriet!" Caroline exclaimed irritably. "He had to sit somewhere!"

"Yes, but he had a good look round first before deciding where to go and he waited till he'd got Mr Lark away from where you were before he sat down at all," Harriet pointed out sagely. "I watched him."

"Well, I think it was very unkind of you! You had no right to be so inquisitive!" Caroline scolded indignantly.

"And you blushed and looked very confused," her cousin chortled gleefully.

This silenced Caroline and she turned her back on her cousin in a huff and began to ponder over her predicament. If she tried to explain her behaviour in the drawing room, for which Harriet had given another meaning, she would have to take her into her confidence; but she felt she would be taking a risk if she disclosed her thoughts and intentions to her cousin. One word, and one word might easily slip out from Harriet's careless tongue, and her schemes would be ruined, not to mention the rumpus there would be when her aunt got to know. But on the other hand if she said nothing Harriet would continue to believe that she was attracted to Sir James Reddaway.

It was exceedingly tiresome and Caroline was beginning to wonder whether she hadn't better explain everything when Harriet's voice broke in upon her reflections again. "Caroline, supposing he is in love with you and asks you to marry him, will you accept him?"

"No, I won't!" Caroline answered curtly and rather grumpily. "I'm not in love with him — in fact, I don't think I like him very much!"

"But you said you did just now!"

"Oh, Harriet, you know what I mean!" Caroline cried in exasperated tones. "I didn't say I disliked him! I meant that he didn't mean anything more to me than anyone else!" She turned aside to the window. "But I wish I hadn't — "

She left the sentence unfinished and Harriet glanced up at her inquiringly. "Hadn't what?"

"Oh, never mind!" Caroline answered evasively.

There was an uncomfortable silence; then Harriet said "Caroline, you're hiding something from me."

After another, longer silence Caroline turned round. "I wish I hadn't asked him to get me that book in Hexham," she muttered in a worried voice.

Harriet's blue eyes opened wide and her small mouth grew slowly into a round, red circle. "Did you ask him to get it for you this morning?"

Caroline nodded her head despondently.

A long drawn-out 'oo-oo' escaped Harriet's lips. "That's just what he wanted!" she chuckled delightedly. "Now you've done it! I can just imagine him singing his way across the moor tonight!"

"Oh, be quiet!" snapped her cousin rudely.

"It's obvious now what he wants," Harriet went on, not a bit put out. "Oh, won't it be wonderful to call you Lady Reddaway!"

"I don't want to be called Lady anything!" was the surly rejoinder.

"You are silly, Caroline! Think how you'll be envied if you marry him!"

"Oh, do stop talking about him!" Caroline implored her peevishly. "I don't want to be envied!" She turned her back on her cousin again and stood in front of the window, biting her lip angrily, her face flushed and passionate, and neither girl spoke for several minutes.

Harriet, though perplexed by Caroline's odd behaviour, was now quite convinced that Sir James Reddaway had every hope of success. She did not know that her cousin's agitation was due to the complications in which she was becoming more and more involved. Of course Harriet might be wrong in her assumption that Sir James was in love with her. But supposing she was right? The very thought made Caroline tremble. Her aunt trying to force her to accept Mr Lark, Sir James urging her to marry him and she not wanting to marry either of them — what a situation for a defenceless girl! And if her aunt got to hear of the second suitor her life would become unbearable. She would be pestered from morning till night every day till she had accepted one of them.

Bitterly did Caroline regret having asked Sir James to bring her the novel. Oh, why on earth hadn't she guessed that there was something behind his little trick to get Mr Lark away from the settee! Certainly, she acknowledged to herself, she had grown to like Sir James better but she didn't think she could ever love him. He was too cold and supercilious and she didn't altogether trust him for he was an enigmatic person. He looked as if he might have a quick temper and she didn't care for the rather caustic way he had of making fun of people. It had been amusing to listen to him ridicule the rector's plan for catching the Midnight Horseman, but she had to admit that he had behaved badly to the young clergyman even though he may have deserved it.

Caroline was so preoccupied that she failed to observe that her cousin was watching her curiously. Nor did she see the mischievous grin on her face. "Caroline — " she began in a tentative tone, " — is there someone else?"

"No, of course there isn't!" Caroline replied shortly, without turning her head.

"Mama thinks there is."

Caroline stiffened with a little jerk and turned round quickly. "Someone else?"

"Yes."

"Who?"

"Mr Lark."

Caroline tossed her head and flung away with an unladylike exclamation of disgust. "Harriet, how can you be so horrid as to mention that odious man! You know what a quarrel Aunt Julia and I had about him this morning!"

"Yes, didn't you!" Harriet giggled. "Goodness, what a bate Mama got into! She thinks Mr Lark would make just the husband for you. 'Tis true he is a bit pompous and conceited but you wouldn't mind that, would you?" she said, smiling angelically up at her cousin.

There was a fiery glint in Caroline's eyes as she swung round and stepped briskly across the room. "I've a good mind to box your ears, you horrid, little tease!" she cried, seizing Harriet by the shoulders and pressing her down into the chair. "You know quite well I would!" she added, giving her squirming victim a vigorous shake by way of emphasis. "I think he's a dreadful man! He never stops talking for a minute and he treats us as if we were the children in his parish school! Poor little things! What they must have to endure!" she murmured sympathetically, releasing Harriet.

"Mama thinks a great deal of him," Harriet said. "That's why she's sending you to Cullaton with Miss Merrilock tomorrow." A thought suddenly occurred to her. "Caroline — I wonder if he'll propose to you then!"

"I shall refuse him if he does."

"I don't think that will discourage him."

"No, I don't suppose it will," Caroline agreed, with a sigh. "He'll think I'm just being modest and it will only make him more persistent."

"If you're not very careful he'll make you give in after all, so you'd better hurry up and marry Sir James," Harriet advised, with a naughty twinkle in her eye. Caroline darted her an angry look and she chuckled wickedly. "How funny Mr Lark looked when Sir James suggested he should go and search for the horseman alone!" she exclaimed. "He wasn't at all brave then!" She gazed thoughtfully into the empty fireplace. "Caroline, I wish we could see him!"

"Who?"

"The Midnight Horseman. It would be fun to see a ghost."

"It would mean going on to Cullaton Moor at night!"

"Oo, I shouldn't like that!" Harriet shuddered.

"Why not? You needn't let him see you."

"Yes, but supposing he is a ghost?" Harriet reminded her nervously.

"A ghost can't harm you," Caroline asserted coolly. She walked slowly back to the window. "Yes, it would be rather fun," she murmured to herself.

Harriet regarded her cousin's back in puzzled silence; then, as a dreadful suspicion began to dawn upon her, a look of alarm spread across her face. "Caroline, you aren't — Caroline, what is it you are contemplating?" she demanded apprehensively.

There was an air of determination about her cousin as she turned and faced her. "You said just now that I wouldn't mind marrying Mr Lark, didn't you? Well, I'm going to prove to you that I'm not the sort of girl who is content to spend her life shut up in a dusty old parsonage. I shall go to Cullaton Moor tonight to watch for the Midnight Horseman," she announced in a decided tone.

"Caroline — no — you mustn't! You dare not do such a mad thing!" Harriet cried in appalled accents, jumping to her feet in consternation.

"Yes, I dare."

"But, Caroline, you mustn't! It isn't safe!" Harriet remonstrated panic-strickenly. "He might find you and — and kill you!" she cried, her voice rising to a wail at this frightful thought.

"I shall only go a little way on to the moor where I can see the crossroads," Caroline reassured her. "I can run away or hide if he comes and anyhow he won't see me in the dark."

"But he might! It's nearly full moon!"

"Good; I shall be able to see him more clearly."

"Oh, Caroline, you oughtn't to do it!" Harriet protested, seeing that she was not to be deterred. "You're bound to get into a scrape and Mama will be dreadfully cross if she finds out! Please don't go!" she entreated.

But Caroline refused to be put off. "I don't care if she does find out," she declared recklessly. "Promise you won't tell anyone?"

Her cousin's stronger will was too much for Harriet and she put her hands over her mouth and giggled childishly. "Yes; but I'm certain you'll be too frightened!" she tittered.

"I shan't!" Caroline retorted resolutely. "I'm going into the garden." And she swept out of the nursery, leaving Harriet gazing after her quite dumbfounded.

As she had neglected her own patch of garden for several days she set to work to tidy it up, snipping off dead blooms and digging up weeds.

The time passed quickly for her as she worked steadily on till her hands were grimy with soil and her usually pale face a deep rosy pink with the heat and exertion.

Pausing at length to contemplate the result of her efforts, she untied the yellow ribbons of her straw hat and pushed it to the back of her head, with a contented sigh. Then picking up her basket and trowel, she sauntered down the path to the hothouses where she found Benjamin.

"How's Jemima?" she asked, climbing nimbly on to the top of a pair of low, wooden steps.

"Ah — 'er's 'ad another kindle o' kittens — third this year!" Benjamin told her, and he sounded almost indignant at the frequency with which his cat brought families into the world.

"How many did she have this time?"

"Three."

"Only three! That's less than usual!"

"'Tis quite sufficient," Benjamin rejoined bluntly.

"What colour are they?"

"Two black and white and one ginger. I'm sure I don't know where — "

He pulled up abruptly and smoothed the back of his hand to and fro across his mouth and then disappeared amongst some chrysanthemums; but when he emerged Caroline was ready with some more questions. "Have you heard any more about the burglary at Court House, Benjamin?"

The old man shook his head.

"Has the Midnight Horseman been seen again?" Caroline tried again.

"Not that I've 'eard."

"I wish I knew someone who had seen him," Caroline sighed.

The watery, blue eyes were turned upon her in an intent, searching scrutiny. "For why?"

"Because I want to know if there really is such a person."

"I shouldn't trouble your 'ead about 'im," Benjamin advised.

"But it would be nice to know the truth about him," Caroline argued, "I wonder how I could find out," she murmured pensively.

The watery, blue eyes were fixed upon her in an even more intent and searching scrutiny. "You not be thinking o' going out yonder yourself'" Benjamin demanded, jerking a horny finger in the direction of the moor.

Caroline gave a start and coloured guiltily at this singularly accurate divination of her thoughts, for, to tell the truth, her questions were prompted by a desire to find out something more positive about the Midnight Horseman before she finally did embark upon her nocturnal expedition on to Cullaton Moor. She wasn't altogether happy about it and felt that she might be risking the perils of the moor and the disgrace of discovery for nothing, because Sir James Reddaway might be right after all, the horseman might be just a myth invented by a few imaginative rustics. But if he wasn't — well, Caroline couldn't help experiencing some qualms at the prospect of being alone in the dark, even on the wide, open acres of Cullaton Moor, with such a sinister, possibly dangerous, character; the wide, open acres might prove to be not quite wide enough and they might also prove to be too open. "Oh, no, Benjamin, of course I'm not!" she lied, with a forced laugh.

"You be wild enough for it," the old gardener asserted grimly.

The auburn ringlets trembled with the husky ripple of laughter that greeted this candid observation. "I shouldn't mind going on the moor if I had you with me, Benjamin," Caroline chuckled.

"Well, you can make up your mind to do w'out me," he retorted tartly. "And don't you be so mad as to go neither, Miss Caroline," he rasped, wagging his grubby forefinger at her. "You'll be getting yourself into trouble if you do," he warned her.

"What's wrong with the moor?" Caroline demanded.

The old gardener shook his head mysteriously. "You never knows," he muttered darkly. "Yon moor, tain't no place to be on after sundown. There be queer creatures about — ah, very queer creatures," he said, with a ponderous shake of his head. "So you take 'eed what you be about now, miss."

"Don't worry, Benjamin. I wouldn't — " Caroline stopped suddenly and a look of consternation spread across her face. "Goodness! There's somebody coming!" She scrambled hastily off the steps and ran towards the door into the garden as the drone of voices outside reached her ears.

But she was too late. To her dismay she saw a stately cavalcade headed by her aunt and Archdeacon Knox proceeding in a leisurely manner down the path to the hothouse. Behind her aunt and the archdeacon came Mr Allen and Mrs Knox and lastly Harriet with Charlotte Knox. As they approached her Caroline could not help feeling that the immaculate appearance of the little party contrasted strikingly with her own dishevelled state. But her retreat was cut off now for there was no way of getting out of the hothouse without being seen and she just had time to smooth down her dress before the archdeacon and Mrs Allen arrived at the hothouse door.

"Ah, there you are, Caroline!" Mrs Allen cried. The next instant she caught sight of the dangling yellow ribbons, the smudged face and the faded straw hat perched askew the profusion of ruffled curls. "Where have you been? We have been looking for you everywhere!" she complained, glaring frostily at her niece.

"I have been working in my garden, Aunt Julia. It was rather untidy," Caroline explained meekly.

"An occupation highly to be commended," the archdeacon proclaimed in his authoritative boom.

Mrs Allen wasn't so sure about this but contented herself with commenting "You should have chosen a better time for your gardening, Caroline. And it is a pity you cannot do it without making yourself look such a sight."

"It is an excellent thing for your people to employ their leisure in a profitable pursuit," Archdeacon Knox observed impressively. "Gardening is a pastime improving to both the body and the mind and I am sure your niece's industry will not be without its reward, ma'am."

"Caroline seems to have been particularly diligent this afternoon," interposed Mrs Knox who had joined them. "You are fond of gardening, are you not, my dear?" she said sweetly.

"Yes, ma'am, very," Caroline replied politely.

"I should like to see your garden," Mrs Knox said, with kindly interest. She bent her head to Caroline's ear. "Perhaps we might desert the others for a little while and then you could show it to me," she suggested softly.

Though she didn't much care for this proposal Caroline couldn't very well refuse; and leaving the others to inspect the hothouses, she took Mrs Knox back to her garden.

"Enchanting! Enchanting!" Mrs Knox gushed, as she surveyed the little plot. "How I envy you it! This little corner must afford you great joy, my dear!"

"Yes, it does, ma'am."

"You must look forward to the day when you have a real garden of your own," Mrs Knox continued, starting to move slowly on up the path.

"I am quite content with the one I have here," Caroline informed her.

"But it would be so much nicer to have a garden entirely of your own, do you not think?"

Caroline sensed the direction Mrs Knox's remarks were leading and resolved to be just as wily. "I hadn't ever thought about it," she answered in a tone of indifference. "My garden here has always given me enough to do."

"But if you had a large garden with a man to work for you, you would have so much more scope for exercising your undoubted gifts in this direction," Mrs Knox pointed out. "And I know a delightful garden that badly needs someone to take care of it. It has a charming house too," she added in a confidential whisper. She glanced covertly at her young companion's face. But Caroline continued to walk calmly along the path, apparently unmoved by this information. "Aren't these roses beautiful!" Mrs Knox exclaimed, pausing in front of a rose bed. "I don't think there is a more perfect flower to be found! Don't you agree, my dear?"

"Yes, they are a very pretty flower," Caroline said laconically.

"The roses in the Rectory garden at Cullaton are very lovely," Mrs Knox remarked casually, as they strolled on again. "I am so glad the new rector is a keen gardener. It would be a great pity if that sweet garden was to be neglected. Have you been over to Cullaton since Mr Lark was appointed to the benefice?"

"No, I have not been yet."

"Oh, you must go soon then!" Mrs Knox declared. "You would be charmed by the garden — and the house too! Everything is so bright and cheerful — I declare I quite envy him such a rectory! It is a perfect residence, commodious, well appointed and in an excellent situation. And its closeness to Chollingford Hall gives its inmates the privilege of acquaintance with the Wrosthdales. Of course I know that the family have not lived there for several years, but I believe that there is every likelihood that the new earl will occupy the Hall. If he does the rector — and his wife — may expect to be honoured with an invitation to the Hall from time to time." She paused a moment and glanced up at the sky. "Mr Lark is a charming young man, do you not think?"

"He seems very amiable," Caroline condescended.

"He has many good points," Mrs Knox resumed swiftly. "Conscientious, kind-hearted and well-bred, he has altogether an admirable disposition." She bent her head a little closer to Caroline. "I think you should know, my dear, that you have made a great impression on him," she confided. "He has told the archdeacon he thinks you one of the prettiest girls he has ever met."

"I am obliged to him for the compliment," Caroline said, albeit a trifle coldly.

"Yes, there can be no doubt he has a high opinion of you," Mrs Knox went on. "Indeed, I think I may say he is greatly attracted by you for it is evident from the way he speaks of you that he admires you a great deal, which, of course, makes me very happy on your account, my dear, because I know only too well how rare eligible young men are these days." She waited to allow time for this to sink in. "You sat next to Mr Lark at Mrs Digby's, I believe?"

"Yes."

"Did you not find him a fascinating person?"

They walked three or four steps before Caroline spoke. "He was quite pleasant to talk to."

"I am so glad you liked him," Mrs Knox purred. "And I feel sure you will come to like him a great deal more when you and he are better acquainted."

Caroline felt she was quite well enough acquainted with Mr Lark to be certain that there was no one she could like less, except possibly the lady with whom she happened to be walking at that moment.

"Here is your aunt!" Mrs Knox cried, espying Mrs Allen and the archdeacon coming up the garden. "I have just been telling Caroline she has an admirer, Mrs Allen," she said gaily. "The Rector of Cullaton is falling in love with her."

"It is a pity Caroline is not more sensible of her good fortune," Mrs Allen observed rather acidly. "I fear she is so particular about her choice of a husband that she is willing to risk remaining single all her life."

Caroline felt so humiliated by his betrayal that she was tempted to gather up her petticoats and rush headlong into the house. And as she stared dejectedly at the ground she was conscious of the eyes of the three of them concentrated on her, as if trying to intimidate her into submission.

"We must give her time to get to know the gentleman," Mrs Knox said kindly. "It is quite right that she should not be too impulsive. But I am certain she will learn to appreciate his many estimable qualities when she is better acquainted with him."

"Your niece is to be commended for her caution, ma'am," the archdeacon said, with a paternal smile at Caroline, "for it will undoubtedly raise her in the estimation of our young friend and make him more eager for success. He must not think to gain too easy a victory. He must prove himself by his pertinacity a worthy suppliant for the lady's hand and heart," he concluded gallantly.

"I think we may depend upon him to do that," his wife laughed as they moved on up the garden. "He will not be easily discouraged."

Nothing further was spoken upon the subject and Caroline followed her aunt and the two visitors back to the house. She was fuming inwardly. That they planned to marry her to the Rector of Cullaton there could be no doubt now; and what was still more infuriating, the Knoxs clearly accepted as certain the ultimate success of their match-making. They'd have to look for someone else then, Caroline muttered to herself. She was by this time in a thoroughly discontented mood and she glowered rebelliously at the archdeacon's long, black back as she followed him into the porch. If they believed they could bend her to their will they were sadly mistaken. She wasn't going to spend her time arranging flowers in Cullaton Church and listening with devoted admiration to Mr Lark's dull sermons. The privilege of acquaintance with the Wrosthdales indeed! It was highly unlikely they'd have much time for an insignificant country clergyman. And if the earl did return he would probably be accompanied by a supercilious countess who would look at the occupants of the rectory with lofty disdain, if she bothered to look at them at all.

As is to be expected, these reflections did not tend to soothe Caroline's turbulent state of mind; rather they only increased her recklessness and made her even more determined to carry out her intention of going to watch for the Midnight Horseman. And she didn't care if she was found out, she vowed defiantly. Perhaps Mr Lark wouldn't be so eager to marry her when he saw what a harum-scarum she was; certainly Mrs Knox would have nothing more to do with her when she heard about it. Well, that would be no great sacrifice. But she wasn't going to be forced into marrying Mr Lark just to please Mrs Knox. It was time someone stood up to her and showed her she couldn't always be managing other people's affairs, Caroline decided firmly.

With such unamiable thoughts passing through her mind it was not surprising that when the Knoxs went to their carriage Caroline could only bring herself to give them a chilly smile and the briefest of curtseys. And as soon as the carriage had left the steps she hurried upstairs before her aunt had time to deliver the reprimand she had intended for her about her appearance.

Chapter Seven

Caroline was in an indeterminate mood as she sat by the open window of her bedroom in the deepening twilight later that evening. One minute she would be assailed by doubts as to the wisdom of her intentions. Then Mrs Knox's complacent smile would pass before her eyes and her doubts were straightaway banished. Peeping through the curtains a moment later, she would see forbidding grey clouds gathering on the darkening horizon, creeping slowly across the violet sky and throwing a mysterious, gloomy obscurity over the silent garden, and her doubts were renewed. But Mrs Knox prevailed; and when, at length, the grandfather clock on the landing struck eleven, she picked up a dark green cloak lying on the bed, hesitated an instant, and then throwing it round her shoulders, she picked up a candle from her bedside table and stepped cautiously out into the long gallery.

She paused, listening intently, and then tiptoed to the head of the wide, oak staircase. The flickering flame of the candle cast sombre shadows on the dark wainscoting and she glanced apprehensively behind her as she crept softly down the thickly carpeted stairs and across the hall to the library where there was a door into the garden. Very gingerly she drew back the iron bolt, and snuffing the candle which she hid beside the door, she pulled it open and stepped out on to the terrace.

The cool night air blew freshly in her face, making her recoil momentarily; but wrapping her cloak closely about her body and pulling the hood over her head, she moved with short, hesitant steps down the path, glancing nervously up at the high box hedges which reared darkly above her on either side, to the gate out of the garden. Hurrying along the lane to Cullaton Moor, Caroline was surprised to find that she did not feel nearly so frightened as she had expected. True her heart was beating furiously, but it was more with excitement than from fear. And now that she was clear of the Grange she became almost light-hearted because she had been more worried about being detected in the act of leaving the house than about the consequences of her escapade. At least she had avoided the ignominy of being stopped and ordered summarily back to her room without having achieved anything at all.

A feeling of exultant, carefree abandon took possession of her when she got out of sight of the Grange chimney stacks, and she began to run down the lane, her small feet pattering on the dry, rutted mud. Above her the sky was becoming more overcast and heavy banks of cloud lumbered monstrously across the moon's face, dimming its cold, silvery light eerily to a deceptive, grey mistiness.

In a few minutes she reached the wooden gate at the end of the lane, and passing through it, she began to climb the wide, open slope of moorland ahead. She pulled the hood of her cloak closer about her head for a keen wind drove into her face from the north. As she ran nimbly over the short grass she lifted her petticoats to avoid the clumps of fading scrub and heather which tore at them, as though attempting to turn her from her purpose. Now and again a stony patch caused her to stumble; but she scrambled on till she gained the higher ground ahead of her, and crossing the last few yards of moorland, she came to the bank below one of the roads across the moor.

She halted, hot and breathless, at the side of the road and peered eagerly about her into the night. To her left she could dimly discern the stark, gallows-shaped outline of the signpost at the crossroads further over towards the south side of the moor, but the clouds were steadily overcoming the moon, making the night hang like a great velvet curtain all around. The uncanny darkness filled her with a sense of loneliness and bewilderment and she had to admit that she was beginning to feel just a little bit afraid.

Baffled by the gloom and silence, she crouched below the bank, one hand pressed into the soft, spongy grass. A stray curl, escaping from beneath her hood, danced lightly on her cheek, blown to and fro by the breeze. She listened intently, hoping to detect something that might warn her that the Midnight Horseman was approaching, but her straining ears could pick up no louder sound than the faint sigh of the wind drifting through the sparse herbage of the moor. Then, away in the distance, the clock in the tower of Cullaton Church began to strike twelve. Caroline counted the deep, measured, sonorous chimes as they came floating slowly and clearly over the quiet moorland, till the last chime died away, leaving her once more with only the dismal moan of the wind in her ears.

Perhaps it was the awful monotony of sound, perhaps it was just fatigue; but after a while Caroline's mood of alert vigilance began to ebb away till at last, passing her hand wearily across her forehead, she sank down against the bank, cold, tired and dispirited. Perhaps after all she was wasting her time. She wasn't by any means certain there was such a person as the Midnight Horseman; and even if there was, he mightn't have chosen this night to ride on the moor; or he might have passed that way already; or he might not be coming for several hours yet, and Caroline didn't feel inclined to stay much longer in that bleak, chilly spot.

Then suddenly, just as she was thinking of going back home, she heard a slight movement quite close to her, a tiny rustle and then a faint metallic clink. She looked up quickly and the next instant sprang to her feet with a terrified gasp, her eyes round with fear. Hardly a yard from her, towering above her like a great statue, stood a huge, black horse with a tall, greatcoated rider on its back.

Caroline drew back instinctively, though she could tell by the inclination of his head that the rider had seen her, and she cowered against the bank in dumb horror, her heart thumping madly against her chest, her eyes transfixed.

He was evidently in no hurry to speak. But after what seemed an interminable length of time, while she waited, indeed, prayed, for him to say something and break the suspense, she heard a quiet, pleasant voice speaking in a slow, rather perplexed, drawl. "Hullo! What have we here? A moorland spirit?"

Caroline was still too petrified to reply and he edged his horse closer and bent down and peered into her white, upturned face.

"A lady — eh!" he exclaimed in surprise. "Well, I be — " He broke off and stared at her in silence. "Are you lost, ma'am?" he inquired politely.

Caroline struggled to make her paralysed tongue work. "N-o, sir," she managed in a feeble croak.

Another pause.

"Then what brings you here at this hour?" A possibility struck him. "But stay — perhaps I should not have asked that question! Maybe I have disturbed a lovers' tryst!"

"Oh, no, sir, you are quite wrong!" Caroline exclaimed impetuously, hastening to correct this misapprehension.

The stranger straightened up slowly. "Well, what the devil are you doing here then? You're not a gypsy, are you?" he questioned in a puzzled tone.

Caroline was in a quandary. She was afraid that if she admitted that she had come to look for him he might think she was spying on him or a decoy sent to lead him into a trap, and a fresh chill of horror ran down her spine at the thought of what might happen to her if he did come to any such conclusions. But if she didn't tell him the truth what possible excuse could she give for her presence on the moor? She gazed helplessly at the tall horse barring the way and decided that it was useless to attempt deception. "I — I — " The words stuck in her throat. "I came to see you!" she blurted out at last.

He smoothed his hand up and down the horse's neck, evidently weighing up this rather lame admission. "Really! And for what reason, may I ask?"

Caroline looked about her in desperation; but flight was out of the question; he could overtake her in a twinkling. "I wanted to see — " she began hesitantly. "I wanted to see if you were a ghost!" Caroline fancied she heard the faintest chuckle.

"I'm sorry to disappoint you, but I confess I'm only just another humble mortal like yourself," he said. He swung his leg swiftly over the horse's back and jumped to the ground. "See," he invited, drawing off his glove and holding out his hand.

The long fingers gleamed palely in the moonlight and, impelled irresistibly, Caroline drew her hand from beneath the folds of her cloak and touched his timidly, letting the tips of her fingers rest for an instant on the smooth, warm flesh.

"Are you satisfied?" he inquired, a note of raillery in his voice.

"Ye-es."

"Is that the sole purpose of your — visit?"

"Oh, yes, sir!"

"I am indeed honoured!" he said, the note of raillery creeping into his voice again. "Are you — disappointed in me?"

"I don't comprehend you, sir," Caroline replied, puzzled.

He laughed softly. "I mean — aren't you sorry to find that I'm not a ghost after all?"

"Oh, no!"

"H'm. Then you prefer to be at the mercy of an unscrupulous vagabond than be face to face with a phantom?"

"I have no choice at the moment," Caroline retorted, her courage beginning to return a little.

"That's very true," he agreed, a suspicion of a chuckle in his voice again. "You are utterly in my power without the smallest hope of escaping or of obtaining help. Doesn't the thought terrify you?"

"A — little."

He was quick to notice the hesitation in her reply. "Ah, your courage falters!" he cried in triumph. "Aren't you afraid that I may cut your throat or hang you on the signpost at the crossroads or — " He lowered his face to hers and gazed deeply into her eyes, a puckish smile on his mouth. In the dim light of the moon Caroline could see that he was young and, she thought, rather good-looking, with a mass of untidy curly hair.

"I — don't think — so," she faltered, drawing back.

"You have admirable spirit then — and confidence. You realise who I am, don't you?"

"Ye — es, I think so."

"Then don't you think you have been very imprudent to have allowed yourself to fall into my clutches?"

"Perhaps."

"You know what people say about me?"

Caroline nodded her head mutely.

"Do you doubt what they say?"

"I don't know," she answered uncertainly. "I wasn't sure you existed — till tonight. Nobody could tell me very much about you."

"But what they did tell you wasn't very favourable?"

"Most people believe you are either a highwayman or a ghost."

"And now you know I'm not a ghost you are convinced that I am a highwayman?"

"N-o — I don't know what to think," Caroline murmured.

"Would you believe me if I told you I wasn't a highwayman?"

Caroline considered this question cautiously before answering him. She couldn't help feeling that appearances were against him; yet apart from the burglary at Court House there was nothing she could hold against him. "I might."

"I wish you would," he pleaded, with an earnestness that surprised her. "You needn't be afraid of me. I shan't harm you," he promised. "Does anyone know you've come here tonight?"

"No, only Harriet," she told him, adding hastily, "but I made her promise not to tell anyone."

"Who is Harriet?"

"My cousin."

"Your cousin?" He regarded her in silence. "Where do you live?"

"At Ullingham Grange."

"Have you lived there long?"

"For twelve years."

"Twelve years," he repeated thoughtfully. "Do your father and mother live there?"

"No; both my parents are dead. Mr and Mrs Allen are my guardians."

"And Harriet is their daughter?"

Caroline was beginning to wonder how much longer this extraordinary interrogation was going to go on. She didn't feel so frightened of him now. His quiet, cultured voice and his gentlemanly manner made him seem much less terrifying. There was a vivacity about him which attracted her and made her long to see his face properly, and she had to confess that she was intrigued by this unknown horseman who had caught her unawares on the moor.

"Now that your curiosity has been satisfied, may I have the honour of escorting you home?" he requested, offering her his arm. "Cullaton Moor is no place for young ladies to be on alone."

"Oh, pray don't trouble! I can quite easily find my own way!" Caroline assured him.

"I shouldn't dream of letting you go back alone," he stated firmly. "Besides, I don't feel inclined to deprive myself of your company so soon," he added lightly. "I shall take you as far as the gate at the end of Ullingham Lane."

There was a note of command in his voice which told her that it would be useless to argue; and accepting his arm, she set off with him across the moor.

They walked on for a while without speaking, the tall horse following them obediently, its hooves thudding dully on the springy turf, till her companion turned to her and said tentatively "Will you tell me your name?" Then seeing her check in surprise, he added quickly "Mine's Charles."

Though amazed at his presumption, Caroline could not feel offended for she detected a sense of diffidence in his voice and she told him her name.

"May I call you Caroline?" he asked.

"It would be foolish of me to object when I am so much in your power," she responded dispassionately.

He looked down at her quizzically. "Are you though? I wonder. I wager that intrepid spirit of yours doesn't yield so tamely — Caroline."

Caroline's face, as she looked up into his, was impassive. "You are very bold, sir."

"I am dealing with a bold woman," he rejoined softly. "Most women in your position would have prostrated themselves at my feet and screamed piteously for mercy. But you — you face me with such unconcern — I might almost say disdain — that no one would credit that I was spoken of in hushed, fearful whispers."

"Perhaps it is because you are not as bad as they say."

"I should like you to think so," he murmured in a sober voice.

Caroline deemed it safest not to be too soft-hearted lest he be encouraged to be even more familiar with her, and they went on again in silence. He was holding her arm and once or twice when she stumbled she felt his strong hand grip hers and prevent her from falling. There was something reassuring and protective about the way he held her up when she faltered so that she instinctively leant on his arm.

When they reached the gate into the lane Caroline turned to thank him. But to her surprise he did not let go of her hand. "I suppose this is where we must say goodbye," he said, rather sadly it seemed to her. "I wish we hadn't to part so soon."

Caroline did not know what to say. Yet she was sorry in a way too for she felt reluctant to leave him, knowing that she might never see him again.

Perhaps her silence gave him a hint of her feelings for he said "Caroline, I admire your venturesome spirit. Dare I — dare I ask you to do what you have done tonight once again? Will you consent to another meeting?"

Caroline was thunderstruck. "Another meeting!" she echoed faintly. "How? When?"

"A week from tonight — here."

"Oh, no, I couldn't!" she objected, drawing back in dismay.

His fingers slowly relaxed their grip of her hand. "You don't trust me then?"

She averted her face. "I don't know." She turned to him again. "Oh, why do you ride the moor at night like this?" she burst out impetuously.

"For no evil purpose I promise you," he responded in a sombre tone.

"But can't you tell me the reason for your strange conduct? How can you expect me to trust you when I know so little about you?"

He let go of her hand altogether. "If you won't trust me why should I trust you?" he retorted coldly. "How am I to know that you won't betray me when you return to your friends?"

"I shan't do that! I should never be forgiven if what I have done was discovered!"

"But how can I be sure that you haven't been sent to lead me into a trap?"

"If that's what you think then it's useless for me to attempt a denial," Caroline rejoined spiritedly, opening the gate.

"I don't think that! I wouldn't have asked you to meet me again if I did!" he flashed out, staying her with his hand. "Tell me — do you know of anything that is to my discredit?"

"They say you broke into Court House?"

"Has it been proved that it was I?"

"No, I don't think so."

"What else am I charged with?"

"Nothing that I know of."

"Then why won't you do what I ask?" he pleaded. "If I had intended you any harm shouldn't I have seized the opportunity when I had it tonight?"

"I suppose so," Caroline acknowledged reluctantly.

The horseman took her hands gently in his. "Look — I'll strike a bargain with you. If I trust you not to betray me, will you meet me here at midnight a week from tonight. If you will dare to come I promise to tell you more about myself then." He stared eagerly into her face as he awaited her decision.

Despite her misgivings Caroline could not bring herself to refuse his request; she was curious to know more about him, and having risked so much tonight, why should she not risk it again? "I will — come," she jerked out; and withdrawing her hands abruptly from his, she darted through the gate and sped off down the lane.

She ran blindly on, staggering crazily as her feet caught in the ruts. She was in a daze, conscious of emotions neither of fear nor elation, so incredible had been the events of the past hour when her self-control had been strained to the limits of endurance; and now that the tension was broken her relief could only be expressed in a wild, headlong dash down the lane.

Reaching the Grange, she crept upstairs to her bedroom, and throwing her cloak on the floor, she flung herself on to the bed, breathless, tired, her hair in wild disarray, but triumphant and deliciously happy.

She had done what she had vowed to do and succeeded beyond her wildest dreams. She had seen the Midnight Horseman — seen and actually spoken to him! She had proved that there was such a man — oh, it was wonderful! What would Aunt Julia and Mrs Knox and everyone say if they knew what she had done! She chortled wickedly and rolled over on her face to stifle the gleeful chuckles the thought evoked. And Mr Lark too! The gallant Mr Lark who had proposed taking a party of armed men on to Cullaton Moor to capture this dangerous marauder — oh, if only she could tell him what she had done! Her body shook with suppressed laughter as she tried to imagine the look on Mr Lark's face. And Sir James Reddaway, the sceptical Sir James who had treated the rumour with such contempt, what would he think of her?

Caroline's hilarity subsided suddenly and she sat up with a thoughtful frown on her face. She had wondered whether Sir James mightn't have been the Midnight Horseman. Well, she knew now that he wasn't. Then who was this mysterious stranger? And what was he doing out on the moor at night? Her heart gave a bound and a startled look shone in her eyes as she recalled the promise she had given, and she slid off the bed and began to undress in a rather subdued mood.

Whatever had possessed her to make such a rash promise? To go out there late at night to meet a man of whom she knew nothing — it was fantastic! But did she know nothing now? Perhaps she did know something of him, enough at any rate to make her want to meet him again. And if he kept his part of the bargain she should be able to learn more about him. Yes, it might be worth it ....

Caroline finished undressing and got into bed. She had a week in which to make up her mind, she reflected drowsily. And she needn't go if she didn't feel like it. But didn't she? Caroline had to confess to herself that she felt a strong inclination to pursue the acquaintance further. Not only was she impelled by a curiosity to find out more about him, but his pleasant voice and humorous, friendly manner gave her a secret thrill, the sort of thrill that brings a blush to a young lady's cheeks, the sort of thrill she loves to feel but refuses to admit. She yawned and pressed her sleepy head into the soft pillows. A week from tonight . . .

Chapter Eight

Sitting in the drawing room with her mother and cousin after breakfast the next morning, Harriet seemed unusually restless; for as she sewed she kept glancing towards her cousin who was in a chair beside the window as if she hoped to attract her attention. But in this she was disappointed, for Caroline kept her head bent over her work, sewing as though her very existence depended upon her industry. Harriet stared at her in an attempt to hypnotise her into looking at her, upset her work basket, dropped her scissors; but all to no purpose; Caroline just would not look at her, and the only return she got for her pains was a reproving frown from her mother, and she finally gave up in disgust and sank back into the corner of the settee with a discontented pout on her pretty lips.

Mrs Allen folded up the letter she had been reading and put it on the table beside her. "Caroline, you have not forgotten you are going to Cullaton today?" she called. Receiving no response to her inquiry, Mrs Allen glanced sharply at her niece. She was sitting with her chin cupped in her hands, gazing dreamily out of the window, completely in the clouds. Mrs Allen cast her eyes despairingly upwards. "Upon my word! Whatever's the matter with the child?" She raised her voice. "Caroline, I am speaking to you!"

Caroline awoke from her daydreaming with a guilty start. "Oh — yes, Aunt Julia?"

"Child, you seem quite distracted! Are you unwell?"

"Oh, no, Aunt Julia! I am quite well!"

"I am relieved to hear that. I was afraid you had contracted a chill through being out in the open too long yesterday," Mrs Allen said. "You will be ready in good time for Miss Merrilock, won't you?"

"Yes, Aunt Julia. I shall not be late," Caroline promised, gathering up her sewing which had dropped on to the carpet.

"I hope you are not unwell," her aunt said, eyeing her dubiously. "Your behaviour has been very strange this morning. I shall have to watch you very carefully."

She returned to her correspondence; and as soon as she was safely absorbed in a letter, Harriet left the settee and strolled casually over to the window. Leaning over her cousin's shoulder, she whispered "Did you see him?"

Caroline shook her head, without looking up, and Harriet's face fell; then she whispered "But you did go?"

Caroline nodded her head in reply this time; but before Harriet could question her further Mrs Allen exclaimed peevishly "What is the matter, Harriet? What are you whispering about?"

Happily for Harriet her mother did not look up from her letter; if she had, her suspicions would undoubtedly have been aroused. As it was Harriet had time to recover her composure and to concoct a convincing falsehood. "I was looking for a piece of lace, Mama, and I wondered whether Caroline had seen it," she explained innocently.

"Well, there is no need for you to whisper about it," Mrs Allen scolded. "It makes me think you have some secret you don't wish me to hear."

"Oh, no, Mama! Only I did not wish to disturb you!" Harriet assured her, even more innocently.

"You had better try and find it at once," Mrs Allen commanded. "You are exceedingly careless about these things." She turned to her niece. "Caroline, it is time you got ready. Miss Merrilock will be here shortly."

Caroline rose obediently and went to put on her bonnet.

When the carriage drew up before the gate of Cullaton Rectory an hour later Mr Lark came bustling down the path, his round face shining with the brightest of smiles, to hand his visitors out and conduct them, with much ceremony, into his house.

There was a damp, chilly atmosphere about the place and an unpleasant mildewy smell hung in the air, making Caroline wrinkle her small nose in disgust as she followed the other two across the ill-lit hall. Enclosed by tall trees and overshadowed by the church, the Rectory was a gloomy and depressing house. The rooms were small and dingy, overcrowded with inelegant and shabby furniture, hideous black oak cabinets and straight-backed Jacobean chairs, and the decorations drab and funereal, green wallpaper in one room, dark brown in another. As she contemplated the limp curtains and faded carpets, Caroline couldn't help reflecting that this was the home to which her aunt and Mrs Knox were so ready to consign her for the rest of her life. She looked in vain for any sign of fresh paint, and as for improvements — well, it was the most dismal place she had been in for a long time.

Blissfully unconscious of the unflattering thoughts passing through his fair visitor's head, Mr Lark conducted the two ladies round his home in high glee, pointing out, for Caroline's benefit, the size and shape of each room, the beauty of the outlook and all the other amenities which contributed, in his opinion, to the perfection of his residence, in all of which he was seconded by old Miss Merrilock who saw no reason to change any of the things which had served her so well; and since she shared the conversation with Mr Lark, Caroline did not find herself called upon to offer more than an occasional brief assent to what was said.

When they had been over the whole house Miss Merrilock expressed a wish to interview Mr Lark's housekeeper. Seeing in this an opportunity of getting rid of the old lady for a while, Mr Lark was only too happy to oblige her and took her down a dim passage to the kitchen where he introduced her to a decrepit old crone named Mrs Bunce. Caroline noticed him whisper something in Miss Merrilock's ear, to which she responded with a smile and a nod, and he turned with an expression of joy on his face and hurried back along the passage.

"Miss Merrilock desires to have a talk with my housekeeper," he explained. "So perhaps you would care to go round the garden?" he suggested, with an affable smile.

As Caroline was beginning to find the atmosphere of the house somewhat overpowering she was only too glad of a chance to get out into the fresh air and she accepted the invitation promptly.

"These roses need tying up," she commented, casting a critical eye upon the roses climbing the wall beside the door.

"Yes, I'm afraid they do," Mr Lark admitted. "But I have been so busy that I have had scarcely a moment to spare. The many pressing duties of my parish leave me little time for gardening," he added, with a pathetic sigh.

Caroline wasn't much convinced by this excuse but she accepted it without comment. "How pretty those roses are!" she cried, running across the ragged lawn to a flowerbed. "They're Perlenas, aren't they?"

"I — er — yes, that is the name, I believe," Mr Lark agreed uncertainly.

"Oh — and these lupins! They are very fine!" Caroline exclaimed delightedly, darting off down the path to a cluster of yellow lupins as the rector approached. "Your marigolds look very well too," she added, bending down to admire them.

"I am glad you like them," Mr Lark said, a trifle breathlessly, as he hastened after her. "I must confess to a partiality for them myself," he confided, with a simper. "I am very fond of all flowers and I wish I had more time to spare for gardening. Now if I had someone — " The sentence was left in the air for Mr Lark found himself addressing his own flowerbed. He turned to look for his companion and found her delving amongst a bed of spinach.

"Your spinach is in excellent condition," she was kind enough to inform him as he came panting up. "But you ought to leave more room between the plants," she admonished.

"Oh, ought I?" Mr Lark was temporarily at a loss for words; then recovering his breath, he began again animatedly. "It is a delicious vegetable, do you not think, Miss Berkley? So wholesome, so nutritious!"

But Miss Berkley wasn't interested in the nutritive value of spinach and had skipped blithely off up the garden to look at some gooseberry bushes. And no sooner did Mr Lark catch up with her than she caught sight of some lettuces and danced off to inspect them.

And so the tour went on, with Caroline doing most of the talking and Mr Lark vainly endeavouring to keep up with her, which was not at all easy since there was no knowing in which direction she might turn at any minute, till the unhappy young man was panting with the unaccustomed exertion and his face glowing with heat. And his temper was becoming frayed too, for he considered it most undignified for him to have to pursue a bashful maiden of seventeen who was actually showing him round his own garden, quite apart from the fact that the pleasant walk for which he had enticed her into the garden was not going according to plan.

However he was granted a respite when they reached the orchard and he was able to walk beside his visitor for a few enchanting minutes.

"You are fortunate in having an orchard, sir," she remarked, favouring him with a ravishing smile.

"Yes, it is pleasant to have one's own fruit," he agreed, bending forward to get a glimpse of the lovely face hidden by the wide curve of a white silk bonnet. "I own I am rather a glutton for apples. They — "

"I adore apples!" Caroline broke in, gazing longingly up into the branches above her head. "Yours look so lovely and ripe, Mr Lark!" she murmured, turning her soft, grey eyes upon him with such a look of wistful pleading that he was quite overcome.

"I should be exceedingly obliged if you would do me the honour of tasting one," he ventured in an earnest tone.

"Oh, no, sir — I couldn't think of it!" Caroline protested.

"But just one! Pray do be so gracious as to try one!" he insisted gallantly.

Caroline looked up into the tree again. "Well — perhaps I might try just one then," she consented shyly.

Mr Lark was beside himself with joy. "If you will be so good as to select one I will pick it for you," he requested.

Caroline let her gaze wander among the branches of the trees around her, and after walking slowly round one tree, she pointed up to one nice, rosy apple. "Please may I have that one?" she asked, with quite entrancing coyness.

Mr Lark stepped forward with alacrity and reached up to an apple.

"No, not that one! The next one!"

"This one?"

"No, the one above it!"

The rector plunged his arm deeper among the leafy branches. He stretched his arm out to its fullest extent but still could not reach the apple. He stood on the tips of his toes, and straining every inch of his five feet and six inches, just managed to get his fingers round it; but as he pulled it the wretched thing slipped out of his grasp and sprang buoyantly up among the branches again. He tried a second and a third time and the same thing happened; the apple seemed quite as resolved to stay on the tree as he was that it should come off.

At last, after the seventh attempt, he gave in to it, and dropping his aching arm, he turned to Caroline who had been watching his struggles with intense interest, her pretty lips parted in just the suspicion of a smile. "I'm afraid I can't reach it," he admitted ruefully.

"Oh, what a pity! It is such a nice one!" exclaimed Caroline regretfully. "Never mind, another one will do just as well!"

But this indirect challenge could not be ignored without loss of prestige and Mr Lark knew it. "Oh, but you must certainly have it!" he cried. "If you will wait while I fetch a ladder you shall have it in an instant!"

Brushing aside Caroline's protests not to trouble himself, he hurried out of the orchard to return shortly, dragging a ladder, which, after a certain amount of clumsy, manoeuvring, he succeeded in planting safely against the tree; and climbing cautiously up, he picked the required apple and brought it triumphantly down to her.

"It is very kind of you," she murmured shyly, giving him such a bewitching smile as she took the apple that he felt ready to climb all the other trees in the orchard for her.

His good humour was restored and he beamed benevolently upon her, feeling that he was at last beginning to make progress; and as they walked back to the garden he was just in the mood for a little pleasant converse. "I hope you have enjoyed your visit," he began.

"Oh, yes, thank you, sir!" Caroline answered politely, but paying more attention to the apple she was eating than the gentleman at her side.

"It has been a great pleasure — and a great privilege — to have been permitted to conduct you round my new home," the rector declared.

"I like seeing new gardens," Caroline remarked artlessly.

This seemed to suggest that his visitor had come to see his garden rather than him, Mr Lark thought, and his heart sank a little. "I am very fond of gardening," he resumed, "and I consider it an excellent recreation. Of course I had no time for it when I was at Oxford so that I cannot pretend to a high degree of proficiency yet," he simpered.

"No, I suppose not," Caroline agreed in a dreamy tone, pausing to glance back down the garden. She turned to him again. "Mr Lark, did you often get drunk at Oxford?"

The Rector of Cullaton stopped dead in the middle of the path, open-mouthed and scarlet, his eyes almost popping out of his head. That a young lady of gentle birth and sheltered upbringing could entertain such indelicate notions was shocking enough; but that she should dare to utter such a word and ask him whether he had often been drunk was almost unbelievable. "My dear Miss Berkley, what a question!" he gasped in appalled tones.

"But I thought all young men at Oxford did that!" she retorted, gazing at him in round-eyed innocence. "Didn't you have lots of riotous parties and things like that?"

"Oh, no, certainly!" the rector denied indignantly. "I fear your conception of university life is a little distorted, Miss Berkley. There were, admittedly, some misguided creatures who wasted their years there in idleness and dissipation, but I assure you that the great number of us employed our time profitably and conducted ourselves as befitted members of such an ancient and venerable foundation."

"And didn't you even get chased by the proctors?"

The ring of disappointment in Caroline's voice warned Mr Lark that his prestige was falling and he made a desperate bid to save it. "I flatter myself I was able to evade their clutches by subtler means," he said, trying to simulate a crafty smile. "I was not so rash as to flaunt my misdeeds before their eyes and invite disciplinary action."

If this implication that the spirit of adventure had once burned in his breast made any impression on Caroline she did not show it, but walked on up the path, a rather blank look on her face.

"Shall we sit down for a few minutes?" suggested the rector when they came to a rustic seat beside the path. "You must be feeling fatigued after so much exercise."

"Yes, I am feeling a little tired," Caroline said dully. "But I should like to go inside. The sun is rather strong."

Mr Lark cast a lingering look at the seat and followed her sadly across the lawn and into the house where they found Miss Merrilock waiting for them in the hall.

"There you are, my dear! I thought you were never coming!" she greeted Caroline brightly. "Have you been entertained well?" she inquired, with an arch glance at the rector.

"Yes, thank you, ma'am," was the composed reply.

"Well, we must be off now if you are ready." the old lady said. "We must not keep the horses waiting."

And shortly after the ladies set off for home, leaving a crestfallen young man leaning over the Rectory gate. He watched the carriage till it passed out of sight round a bend in the road and then returned disconsolately into the house. The afternoon had not been a success so far as the Rector of Cullaton was concerned.

When Caroline got back to the Grange she was met by an excited Harriet as she crossed the hall. "Oh, Caroline you've missed such a lot this morning! We've had two visitors while you've been out!" she informed her in breathless haste.

"Who?"

"Tom Hawley and Sir James Reddaway!" Harriet babbled on happily. "Tom has offered to teach me to ride! Mama has said I can and I'm to start on Wilfred tomorrow!"

Caroline congratulated her on her good luck and waited to hear more about the callers.

"He stayed quite a long time — in fact till Sir James came," Harriet proceeded volubly, as they went upstairs to Caroline's bedroom. "Oh, but he was disappointed you weren't in!"

"Who — Tom?"

"No, silly — Sir James, of course!" Harriet laughed. "When Mama told him you weren't at home he looked quite put out."

Caroline walked slowly over to the dressing table and untied the ribbons of her bonnet. "Did he say he had come to see me?"

"No; but he only stayed a few minutes when he knew there was no chance of seeing you."

"Did he — " Caroline checked herself. Had Sir James brought her book Harriet would surely have told her. "Did he give any reason for calling?"

"Oh, he pretended he wanted to see Papa about parish business," Harriet replied. "But I don't believe that's what he really came for," she declared sceptically.

Their conversation was interrupted at this point by Mrs Allen's voice calling from the gallery.

"There's Mama calling you!" She wants to hear about your visit to Cullaton," Harriet hazarded.

"Oh, I can't come now!" Caroline exclaimed fretfully. "Tell her I've got a headache!"

The faithful Harriet went off to deliver this message to her mother and Caroline lay down on her bed, thankful that the inevitable interrogation had been deferred at least for a while.

Chapter Nine

Finding her niece reluctant to discuss her visit to Cullaton, Mrs Allen summoned her to the privacy of her dressing room one evening in order to question her more closely. But the interview was not a success. When asked her opinion of the house, Caroline declared it to be dirty and damp; the garden, it was neglected and too shady. When Mrs Allen tried to find out what they had talked about, she was informed 'nothing in particular'; and when pressed for a more exact answer Caroline conceded that they had talked about flowers and vegetables. Such an unenterprizing way of spending a half-hour with an eligible young bachelor did not satisfy Mrs Allen, who then demanded to know whether Mr Lark had shown Caroline any particular attention. Caroline replied that he hadn't, though she didn't reveal that it was because he hadn't been given the chance. Finally, in desperation, Mrs Allen asked whether she found the gentleman improved on acquaintance. Upon being informed that he did not, Mrs Allen lost her temper and declared that she was a foolish, headstrong, ungrateful girl and deserved no pity if she died an old maid; and finding that this dreadful prospect made no impression on her but rather made her more sulky and mulish, Mrs Allen dismissed her with the parting shot that she had no patience with her and would have nothing more to do with her.

With relations between aunt and niece being thus somewhat strained, it was perhaps a good thing that Mr and Mrs Allen had an engagement which took them out for the day on the Saturday of that week; and the cousins agreed that this was a good opportunity for them to do some shopping in Emberhope without first having their purchases sanctioned by Mrs Allen.

They had just come out of Miss Gregson's millinery shop opposite the green and were sauntering slowly up the street when a jovial voice hailed and they turned to find Tom Hawley coming up behind them.

"Good morning, ladies!" he greeted them, with an exuberance that made the geese ambling across the green amble a shade faster. "And what brings you out so early in the day?"

"We have come to do some shopping," Caroline told him.

"And Mrs Allen — has she come too?"

"No, she has gone to Alnwick with Mr Allen."

"Alnwick!" He pursed his lips and uttered a slight whistle. "So you're all alone for the day?"

"Yes."

"How nice for you!" He threw a sidelong glance at Harriet. "And have you been making extensive purchases, Miss Allen?" he inquired, peeping cautiously round the wide brim of her bonnet.

"If it is of any interest to you I have been buying some pink ribbon."

"It is of very great interest to me," Tom assured her. "I shall look out for it in church next Sunday."

Harriet looked up into his laughing blue eyes and surrendered. "May I ask what you are doing idling about the town at this time of the day?"

"I brought a horse in to be shoed and I've got to hang about till he's ready."

"And how do you intend filling in the time?"

"Oh, I shall probably go over to The Crown for a chat and some refreshment," Tom said carelessly.

"You're not going to drink that nasty stuff?" Harriet exclaimed in disgust.

"What else is there for me to do? Unless — some kind young ladies would take pity on me and allow me to share their company for a while," he ventured diffidently.

"I think that would be better than drinking ale in a horrid old inn," Harriet retorted primly.

"So do I," agreed Tom readily.

They strolled on, chatting happily together, till they reached the bridge outside the town.

"You two walk too slowly for me," Caroline said, as they loitered beside the parapet. "I'm going on ahead. I want to do some gardening before it gets too hot." And quickening her pace, she set off up the road out of the town, leaving the other two sauntering hand-in-hand along the river bank.

As soon as she was out of sight of Tom and Harriet Caroline began to stroll in a more leisurely manner along the grass verge. Now and again she stopped to lean on a gate and breathe in the rich, woody fragrance of a hayrick or loitered under the cool shade of the overhanging trees through which the bright shafts of sunlight glinted, dappling the road in light and shadow.

So absorbed was she in her surroundings that it was not until she was within sight of the Grange gates that she became aware that she was being followed. The click of a horse's hooves brought her out of her daydreams, and glancing carelessly over her shoulder, she saw a gentleman on a bay horse. As she turned away she suddenly realised that there was something familiar about the lean, erect figure in the plum-coloured coat and she stopped and looked back again; her heart gave a jerk as she recognised Sir James Reddaway.

Seeing her pause, he urged on his horse and caught up with her. "I had hoped I might find you in today," he began, raising his hat. "You were unfortunately out when I called with the book you asked me to get for you."

As two days had passed since he had called Caroline had convinced herself, wilfully, that he hadn't got the book for her, and it came as an unpleasant shock to her to find that she was mistaken so that she couldn't at once think of anything to say.

"You didn't think I had forgotten it, did you?" he said, with a smile.

"Oh, no, sir! I thought perhaps you had been unable to obtain it!" she stammered in some confusion.

"The bookshop was the first call I made when I reached Hexham," he told her, dismounting from his horse. "May I walk up to the house with you? Abby could do with a rest."

Caroline had to accede to this request, and as they walked into the drive she was conscious of a horrid, sinking feeling within her, because it was clear from his dilatory manner that Sir James had no engagement to prevent him spending a few minutes in the Grange drawing room; and that was the very thing Caroline wished to avoid. But before she knew where she was they were alone in the drawing room. As she sat down on the settee she prepared to entertain her visitor to the best of her ability, knowing full well that there wasn't the least hope of Harriet returning in under an hour.

"I had better give you your book before I forget," Sir James said, handing her a neatly-wrapped package.

"I am most grateful to you, sir, for your trouble," Caroline replied as she took the package from him.

"It was no trouble — rather it was a pleasure," he returned in his quiet, grave voice. "Won't you open it?" he invited, seeing that she did not immediately unwrap the book.

She untied the cord and withdrew the book. It was bound in brown leather with gilt-edged leaves, rather more costly than she had intended to buy, and her eyes lit up with delight as she held it up. "What a beautiful copy!" she cried. "Oh, thank you, Sir James! I am thrilled with it!"

"I hope you will find great enjoyment in reading it," he said, smiling at her unaffected joy.

"Oh, I shall!" Caroline assured him, carried away by the sight of the longed-for book. "I cannot thank you enough! It was most kind of you!"

"It has given me great happiness to have served you in this small way," he said quietly, "and the rapture with which my small gift has been received is ample recompense for my trouble."

The word 'gift' struck a chord in her mind and her look of joy vanished abruptly. "Oh — I was forgetting! Sir James, you must tell me what I owe you for this book so that I may repay you for it!"

"Nothing. Nothing at all."

"But, Sir James, I must! I cannot accept it if you won't let me pay for it!" she protested.

He took a quick step towards her. "Please don't say that! I would like you to accept it as a token of my profound admiration for a very beautiful woman."

Caroline felt the blood rush to her cheeks and she stared up into his face as he bent over her, her eyes wide with astonishment.

"Caroline, it's useless for me to hide it any longer!" he burst out urgently. "I love you! I have loved you ever since I first met you! Every minute of the day I am thinking of you!" To her dismay he sat down beside her and before she could stop him he had seized her hands in his. "Caroline, I have come here today with one purpose alone, to declare my love for you and to ask you to be my wife!"

She was so astounded by this precipitate proposal and by the intensity of his passionate outburst which was so unlike him that she had scarcely the strength to utter a word.

"I don't ... know ... what ... to say," she murmured inarticulately, averting her eyes. "This is most unexpected."

"Can you not say that you love me?" he prompted gently.

She jumped to her feet in great agitation and tried to withdraw her hand but he held it fast. "Oh, please let me go, sir, I beg of you! You are too sudden!" she cried, turning on him almost angrily.

"But, Caroline, think of all I have to offer you! Wealth, rank and my deepest, sincerest affection — all, all shall be yours if you will consent to be my wife!"

"But I have nothing to offer in return," she replied in a low, controlled voice.

"But you have! You have your own dear self! What more could any man desire?" he argued excitedly.

Caroline's head was in a whirl and she could not bring herself to answer him at once. But taking a firm grip on herself she said "You are most kind, sir, and I am deeply sensible of the great honour you do me but — " her voice sank to a whisper, " — I cannot accept your proposal." She dared not look at him, knowing that her refusal was bound to have come as a shock to him.

There was a tense silence; then he stood up. "I see I am too fiery for your gentle nature," he said, with a sigh, moving away from her. He turned round and began again with renewed fervour. "But, dearest girl, give yourself time to reflect! I don't ask for an immediate answer, but don't, I entreat you, reject me out of hand! For weeks now I have been your most ardent admirer — you cannot have failed to notice that! Won't you permit me to offer myself and all that I possess to you for your future happiness?"

The more impassioned he became the cooler Caroline became and his persistence only made her more determined to withstand him. "If I have unintentionally given you reason to hope that your feelings might be returned I am deeply sorry for it," she said, speaking in a mild and collected manner. "I have no wish to give you pain but I do not feel that the strength of my regard for you can ever be more than that of a friend."

If she hoped that was the end of the matter she was disappointed; for the baronet seized her hands and pulled her round to face him again. "Grant me one concession, I implore you! Will you allow me to come to you and repeat my offer when you have had time to consider it?"

But Caroline wasn't going to risk showing any sign of weakening now and she merely replied! "I cannot say any more than I have, sir. Please let us not prolong this conversation. It distresses me much."

"But — "

"No, sir, I have no wish to pursue the matter. You must excuse me." And she ran out of the room, leaving him to find his own way out.

Most girls of her age would have been highly flattered at having two rival suitors. But Caroline, as she sought the sanctuary of her bedroom, experienced no glow of pride or sense of elation; for though she had evaded Mr Lark's clumsy attempts to make love to her and had repulsed Sir James, she knew that neither was likely to leave it at that, the former because he was too obtuse to realise that he would never be accepted and the latter because he was not the sort of man who would lightly abandon something he had set his heart on. It must have cost him dearly to have humbled himself before her as he had and he would not be inclined to have his sacrifice thrown away without a struggle. She knew, too, that so far from expecting sympathy from her friends she would almost certainly be censured for her folly in having rejected two aspirants for her hand. The thought of what her aunt would say if she ever heard that she had rejected the baronet made Caroline cover her face with her hands. It would be the storm of storms! But what was the use if she didn't love him?

She knelt on the window seat and gazed despondently out of the window. Oh, how difficult life had suddenly become! Every day she seemed to get more and more entangled in a web of complications which compelled her to have recourse to deception and secrecy. She had to avoid Mr Lark and Sir James and she had to prevent anyone, but especially her aunt, finding out that Sir James had proposed to her; not that that should be difficult since he was unlikely to disclose her rejection of his proposal. But if he persisted, and it was obvious he would, then there might be no hiding it. Harriet had guessed the truth and so might others too, and Caroline foresaw more trouble in store for her, Sir James's insistency, her aunt's angry reproaches, and just where it would all end Caroline trembled to think. Bitterly did she regret ever having asked for the book that had given the baronet just the opportunity he had been waiting for.

Her gloomy meditations were interrupted by a knock on the door and Harriet entered, without waiting for an answer. "Has Sir James Reddaway been here?" she demanded directly.

Caroline nodded her head and moved across to the dressing table.

"What did he want?"

"He brought the book I asked him to get me in Hexham," Caroline told her, opening a drawer and pretending to look for a handkerchief.

Her cousin's heightened colour and evasive manner had not escaped Harriet and she had a strong inclination to find out the reason for them. "Is that all?" she persisted.

"Ye-es."

Harriet contemplated her cousin's back in silence. "Did he stay long?"

"He came in for a few minutes."

"Then you were alone with him?"

"Yes."

"Oh."

While Harriet was considering her next question Caroline went over to the wardrobe and took out a bonnet.

"Where are you going?" Harriet asked in surprise.

"Into the garden."

"But it's nearly time for lunch!"

"There's a few minutes yet," was the curt response. And quickly tying on her bonnet, Caroline left the room before Harriet had time to ask any more awkward questions.

As she ran down the gallery she almost collided with one of the housemaids. The girl's face was ashen and there were tears in her eyes. "Belinda! Whatever's the matter?" Caroline exclaimed.

"Oh, Miss Caroline — " Belinda hid her face in her hands. "Oh, 'tis dreadful! A man has been murdered on Cullaton Moor!" she blurted out between sobs. "They say the Midnight Horseman must have killed him!"

Chapter Ten

It was a fine, cloudless night when Caroline set out for her assignation on Cullaton Moor, but as the moon was on the wane and the lane was overshadowed by high hedges and trees she couldn't have hurried even if she had wanted to. But for an occasional rustle when some animal bounded through the undergrowth scarcely a sound disturbed the terrifying stillness of the quiet countryside.

Reaching the gate at the end of the lane, she pulled it open a few inches, and peering cautiously forward on either side, she stepped out on to the rough track which ran along the edge of the moor. Almost at once she heard her name called softly. "You see — I have kept my promise," the horseman whispered.

"So have I," rejoined Caroline, drawing away from the tall figure beside her.

"'There's an empty cottage down here where we could go for shelter," he suggested, pointing along the track.

Caroline hesitated for an instant. Then she allowed him to take her hand and lead her down the stony track to a tumbledown dwelling. The horseman guided Caroline through a gap in the tottering wall encircling the cottage and up the narrow, grass-choked path. Pushing open the door, he drew her inside into a low, flagged room lit by a lantern which hung from a beam in the cracked and smoke-grimed ceiling. The place was bare and the single window was covered by wooden shutters, thickly draped with dust and cobwebs.

As the horseman closed the door and turned towards her Caroline stepped quickly across to the far side of the room. He stood still under the lantern, perplexed by her defensive attitude. "I am honoured," he said, with a bow, taking off his hat and gloves. "I was afraid you might change your mind and decide not to come after all."

"I promised you I should," she replied calmly, though inwardly she was feeling anything but calm.

A faintly derisive smile stole across his face. "Yes — but an hour's reflection in the privacy of your bedchamber might have cooled your venturesome spirit," he teased.

"I'm not afraid, if that's what you mean," Caroline retorted.

His eyebrows went up a shade and the smile on his lips widened. In the dim light from the lantern she could see that he was tall and strongly built, with well-defined, bronzed features, unruly, gold-brown hair and a pair of humorous, grey eyes.

"Then why do you retreat from me? Why do you make your distrust of me so plain?" he said.

"Why should I trust you when I know so little about you?" she countered boldly.

"Your prudence is to be commended," he observed drily. "Yet you are ready to risk meeting me a second time."

"Did you not dare me to come?"

The laughter faded from his face and he spoke in a gentler tone. "Yes, and I am infinitely grateful to you." He contemplated her unyielding figure and then said pleadingly "Must we talk with this — " he gestured to the space between them, " — unfriendly gap between us? Won't you tell me what is on your mind?"

Caroline knew that the crisis had been reached at last. She gripped the folds of her cloak to try to stop herself trembling and drew a deep breath. "Last week — a crime was — committed on the moor — " Her courage failed her and she faltered.

The horseman remained quite still but she felt his unwavering scrutiny boring through her. "You mean — the murder?" he prompted softy.

Her 'yes' came in a weak, throaty whisper.

"Well, what of it?"

"Do you — do you know who did it?" she asked haltingly.

He relaxed and turned away. "I know who did it — yes."

Caroline could not stifle the gasp of horror which escaped her lips and she stared at him aghast.

"I understand. You believe I had something to do with this man's death, in fact, that I actually killed him?" He shrugged helplessly. "Well, 'tis natural, I suppose. Everyone else thinks so."

"What do you expect?" Caroline challenged plaintively.

The horseman swung round, his face hard. "Do you believe me guilty of murder?"

They stared deeply into each other's eyes for a moment; then she shook her head, her murmured reply barely audible.

She half-expected to see a smile of triumph or at least of relief appear on his face, but his features remained inflexible as he said "Caroline, I give you my word that I did not kill the man nor had I anything to do with the crime."

"Yet you say you know who did kill him."

"Yes."

"Are you going to do nothing to bring him to justice?"

"I shall do everything in my power," he answered grimly. His face softened and he held out his hands to her. "But, Caroline, won't you come nearer the light? We can't see each other very well like this." Caroline moved slowly towards him. He looked down into her upturned face and then gently pushed back her hood. "You're very lovely!" he murmured. "How old are you?"

"Nearly eighteen."

"Nearly eighteen!" he echoed wonderingly. A tiny smile played round the corners of his mouth and he said "Don't you think you're very rash to trust your life in my hands when you know so little about me?"

"I came tonight because you promised to tell me more about yourself," Caroline reminded him.

"Is that — the only reason why you've come?"

She lowered her eyes. "What other reason could there be?"

He regarded her in silence; then he said "Have you still faith in me?"

She raised her eyes to his again and nodded her head.

"Very well, then; now I shall fulfil my part of the bargain," he continued. "I am, as you have guessed, the man whom some call the Midnight Horseman. My real name I shall not tell you yet because I have a foe who wouldn't scruple to force you to reveal my identity to him if he thought you knew it. My business concerns something of greater consequence than men's purses." He looked at her intently. "Will you promise me faithfully not to breathe a word of it to anyone if I tell you what it is?"

"Yes, I promise — faithfully!" Caroline declared energetically.

"Not even to Harriet?"

"No, not even to Harriet," she smiled.

"It concerns the safety of this country, the safety of England."

"The safety of England!" Caroline repeated in astonishment.

"Yes. The war with France isn't over yet because Napoleon is planning to return to renew the struggle. And throughout Europe his agents are spying and intriguing so that when he makes his bid to recover his lost empire he will know best where to strike." His voice dropped to a lower note. "And one of those agents is here — in Northumberland."

An involuntary gasp escaped from Caroline and he continued.

"Napoleon needs all the information he can get about the strength and whereabouts of our armies and naval squadrons. There have been several instances of leakages of confidential information which have tended to cast suspicion on this man and I have been sent here to try and lay him by the heels. This is a perfect spot to work from because he can use the smugglers' boats which operate along the coast. When I have dealt with this fellow I promise you that you shall know my name. Till then I want you to trust me and keep my secret. Will you?"

Caroline nodded her head mechanically, spellbound for the moment by his narrative. "Oh, yes, I do trust you! I will keep your secret whatever happens!" she burst out, with sudden fervour.

"I am proud to be considered worthy of your trust," he said gravely. "I own I didn't expect you to come tonight though I allowed myself to hope that your courage wouldn't desert you. I shall always remember this night and I hope it won't be long before we meet again." He put on his hat and gloves. "You must go home now. It's getting late and I've work to do before dawn."

A look of fear crossed Caroline's face for there was an ominous ring about the word 'work'. "Is there danger in it?" she questioned anxiously.

The horseman drew her hood over her head and his fingers caressed her cheeks momentarily. "You mustn't worry about me" he said gently. "Haven't I promised you we shall meet again soon?"

"Yes; but how can I be easy when I know that your life may be in danger?"

His eyes were tender as he gazed down into her pale, earnest face. "Does it matter so much to you?"

She nodded dumbly. "They're all trying to trap you and — oh, please let me help you? I'd like to share your danger with you!" she pleaded.

But he was adamant. "I couldn't let you do that," he replied. "Come now — we must — " He pulled up abruptly, his head cocked, alert and tense. "What's that?" He went to the door and opened it slightly. There was a moment of strained silence; then it was broken by a sound, distant but sinister, that sent a chill of fear through Caroline, and her companion turned to her with a grim look. "We've got to get away from here quickly!" he snapped tersely. "They've put dogs on my track!"

Extinguishing the lantern, he took her hand and drew her across the threshold of the hovel. Outside in the darkness the deep, drawn-out baying of hounds came to them again, now frighteningly close in the still night air. The horse whinnied softly and pawed the ground nervously. The horseman whispered reassuringly in its ear, and taking the bridle, began to move towards the track.

"No — wait!" Caroline exclaimed, putting her hand on his arm. "You must go at once! I can find my way alone!"

"But I can't possibly — "

"It doesn't matter about me!" she interrupted swiftly. "But you haven't a moment to waste!"

"No, we go together," he stated firmly, moving forward.

"No, no, we mustn't be found together!" Caroline insisted urgently. "I haven't far to go and they won't notice me in the darkness!" She pressed his arms imploringly. "Please do as I say! It's the safest!"

He contemplated the bright eyes gazing wistfully up at him for a few seconds. "You're a brave woman. I shan't forget this." He raised her hand to his lips and kissed it. "We shall meet again soon. Till then — *au revoir*."

Their eyes dwelt lingeringly on each other for one last instant; then he let go her hand and swung himself agilely on to his horse. At a whispered command from its master the animal wheeled round and climbed the grassy bank and in a second they were swallowed up in the black gloom that enveloped the moor. Caroline stared anxiously after them for a while and then began to make her way back to the lane.

But precious time had been wasted. She had hardly gone a dozen yards when the baying of hounds was repeated, this time much nearer. The horrible moaning unnerved her and she stopped dead in dismay. If she went on she might fall into the hands of the search party and the consequences of such discovery could not be, as she knew full well, anything but disastrous for her.

In her panic she was reminded of the empty cottage. The searchers would probably strike deeper into the moor, she thought as she turned and ran back the way she had come, and if she waited a while she could sneak back to the lane later on.

But as she retreated inside the baying grew louder and fiercer, making her doubt the wisdom of her decision. Oh heavens, if they came here! She stood with straining ears and taut nerves, her heart thumping madly. There was silence for a minute or two. Then there came a thud on the door which made Caroline jump back with fright, followed by a series of low, impatient growls, and she knew she was lost.

After a torturing moment of suspense she heard voices outside and the latch was lifted and a tall, greatcoated man entered. He carried a lantern and his other hand gripped the collar of a huge dog which strained forward towards Caroline. She could not discern his features at first, but then, as he raised the lantern above his head, she realised, with a dreadful sickening feeling, that it was someone who knew her — in fact the last person she wanted to meet — it was Sir James Reddaway.

Appalled by this catastrophe, she stood frozen with horror, her mouth open, a dry, choking sensation gripping her throat.

Sir James looked equally startled and gaped at her in incredulity.

"My dear Miss Berkley, whatever are you doing here?"

"I — I — " She tried to avoid his eyes. "I was taking shelter," she muttered lamely.

"But why are you out in the middle of the night?" he persisted in bewilderment.

Caroline ran her tongue over her dry lips, racking her brains for a plausible explanation. "Harriet dared me to go on the moor at night and I came to prove to her that I wasn't afraid to."

"But, Caroline, how could you be so foolhardy! It's madness to expose yourself to the perils of the moor!"

"I've only been to the edge, Sir James," she defended herself.

"But not an inch of it is safe!" he remonstrated. "And how could you think of venturing on it after what has happened? Why — you might have fallen into the hands of the Midnight Horseman himself!"

Caroline looked at him in surprise. "I thought you didn't believe there was such a person, Sir James!"

"I admit the story seemed fantastic at first," he owned stiffly. "But now that I have seen tangible proof of the reality of the man I have no longer any doubts about him. He's certainly real — only too real," he concluded grimly.

"You think that he — " Caroline deemed it wisest not to discuss the murder and she said, with feigned unconcern. "But I didn't intend to stay out long and I wouldn't have let him see me."

"Yes, I do think he murdered that man," Sir James said in a sombre tone. "That's why I'm so disturbed to find you here. He's such a cunning rogue that you never know where you may encounter him. He might appear beside you without a moment's warning."

Caroline couldn't help thinking that it was rather odd that the one person who had refused to believe in the Midnight Horseman should now hold such very positive views about him. "But I have not fallen into his hands so there's nothing to worry about," she said lightly, going towards the door. "I shall go home now. Please don't tell anyone you found me here, Sir James. My aunt would be very angry if she heard."

"Wait! You cannot go alone!" he objected, barring her way. "I shall escort you!"

Ignoring her protests, he went out with the dog and Caroline heard him speak in a low tone to someone outside.

He returned a moment later alone. "I didn't want anyone to see you," he explained, offering her his arm. He paused suddenly, his glance attracted by something on the floor. Then he turned to her with a curious look. "How long have you been in here?"

His abrupt change of manner made Caroline uneasy and she struggled to keep calm as she answered him. "Not very long."

"Was there — anyone with you?"

"No."

His dark eyes scanned her face suspiciously. "Are you sure?"

"Yes, of course!" Caroline felt herself being mesmerised under the inexorable scrutiny of those intense eyes.

"I am loth to insult a lady," he murmured. "But I confess I'm a trifle perplexed. I cannot comprehend what could bring you out on this desolate moor unless — unless it was that you had an appointment with someone."

"Sir James!"

"Well, what else could it be? No sane person would wander about Cullaton Moor after nightfall without a very good reason."

"I've told you my reason for coming."

"Oh, I know!" he rejoined coolly. "But your visit appears to have coincided with someone else's." He pointed to one of the stone flags. "Do you see that footprint?"

Caroline strove frantically to retain her composure in the face of this terrible crisis as she followed the direction of his finger towards the dark telltale blotch on the dusty floor, knowing very well that his alert eyes were watching her closely. "I don't see what that has to do with me," she parried.

"No?" He pursed his lips and surveyed her through narrowed eyes. "It seems that you have been near this place for some time tonight. Somebody has been in here quite recently because there are traces of a man's boots on the floor. Did you see anyone on the moor?"

"No."

"And no one was with you?"

She rounded on him stormily. "Sir James, why am I subjected to this interrogation? It is most disagreeable to me!"

A queer little smile flickered over his sallow features. "I apologise most sincerely for distressing you." His tone was bland. "But you must understand that I am trying to capture an utterly ruthless criminal and it is my duty to examine every clue most carefully." He leant his face closer to hers. "And you, my dear Caroline," he said in a silky whisper which sent a thrill of fear through her body, "are not a very convincing witness."

"Sir James, you are being most offensive!"

"No — you mistake me!" he cried, throwing up his hands protestingly. "I am merely trying to serve the common cause by apprehending this scoundrel who has aroused widespread alarm throughout the countryside," he lowered his voice again, "and I earnestly beseech you to help me."

"I cannot help you, sir."

He regarded her resolute face for an instant; then he said, quite kindly "Don't you think your compassion is a trifle — ill-judged?"

"I don't understand you, sir," Caroline replied coldly.

"I mean — aren't you shielding a felon simply because you pity him as you would a fox hunted by the hounds?"

She drew back in well-feigned astonishment. "Sir James, your behaviour is incomprehensible!"

"So is yours!" he rejoined softly.

They faced each other in tense silence, he cool and smiling, she pale and dogged, each challenging the other to surrender.

But though her heart was racing madly and her mind was in a wild tumult of fear and anger, Caroline was determined not to give in. "If you have no further questions, sir, I shall be obliged if you will allow me to return home," she said in a tone which was intended to show that the conversation was ended.

He gave her his arm, without a word, and conducted her out of the cottage and along the track to the lane end. In spite of her protests that he need not accompany her up the lane he insisted on going with her, and she had to submit to being escorted right up to the garden gate as though she were his prisoner, for not for a moment did he relax his hold on her wrist. Not only was she humiliated by this miserable anticlimax to what had been an exhilarating adventure, but she was seriously perturbed about the possible sequel to it. Sir James's evident disbelief in her explanation made her view the future with considerable disquiet, which was not lightened by the recollection that a rejected lover was unlikely to have much compassion for the lady who had turned him down. He would do his utmost to drag the truth from her and, as a last resort, he could threaten to betray her to her guardians. And then . . . She closed her eyes, not daring to picture the terrible scene that would follow the exposure of her hoydenish escapade.

When they reached the garden gate he opened it for her, but as she stepped through the gateway he pulled her round so that she was compelled to look at him. "Don't, I beg of you, ever do again what you have done tonight," he whispered. "There is not a more treacherous rogue on earth than the Midnight Horseman. And — " he put his face so near to hers that he was almost touching her, " — he was close, very close to you tonight. Good night."

He released her wrist and she flung away from him without a word and disappeared up the garden in a flurry of skirts, leaving him looking after her, an odd little smile playing on his thin lips.

Towards dawn, some hours later, the Midnight Horseman was sitting in a corner of the oak settle before the fire in the kitchen of The Fox and Hounds, a lonely, little inn at Quigley Cross to the north of Cullaton Moor. He was placidly smoking a long-stemmed, clay pipe while he listened to the young man standing on the hearth.

"The coastguard at Narraton Head reported that he saw a merchantman lying off the coast there early yesterday morning," he said. The mist prevented him from getting a clear view of her, but he thinks she may have sent a boat inshore and then sheered off."

"We'll have to keep a close watch on our friend," the horseman said. "He may be planning a trip to the Continent shortly. He has a hide-out at the old mill at Ocklebridge. I followed him there a few nights ago. That's where he receives his messengers."

"The man who was murdered was one, wasn't he?"

"I imagine so."

"Why do you think he killed him?"

"He was probably untrustworthy; that's usually the reason. He may also have thought to hamper me by putting the hue and cry on to me. He's guessed somebody's after him and he'll quit the country as soon as he can." He stood up and stretched sleepily. "And that, my dear Anthony, we have got to prevent at all costs."

Chapter Eleven

It was with a troubled heart that Caroline went down to breakfast in the morning. She had felt all along that her recklessness would land her in serious trouble sooner or later, but in her eagerness to satisfy her curiosity about the Midnight Horseman she had been blind, wilfully no doubt, to the risks she was running. Harriet had been right when she had foretold that she would get into a scrape; she had, and a frightful scrape it was too! One word from Sir James and she would be ruined. The very fact that she had been found alone on Cullaton Moor at night would be enough to damn her in the eyes of most respectable people, so that it wouldn't matter very much if he did declare his suspicions.

However nothing occurred to ruffle the tranquillity of the Grange household on that day or the next; and when three days passed without the expected storm breaking and without a visit from Sir James Reddaway, Caroline's apprehensions began to die down. Nothing was seen or heard of the Midnight Horseman either, and since the magistrates' investigations into the murder brought little information of value to light, interest in it began to wane; and then came an item of news which quite pushed the murder into the background for the time being.

On the Friday of that week it was announced that Tom Hawley was to marry Harriet Allen. As soon as the young man had had the all-important interview with Mr Allen, Mrs Allen ordered the carriage and rode into Emberhope to receive the felicitations of the archdeacon's wife.

Later, while making some trifling purchases in Miss Gregson's, she was lucky enough to meet Miss Merrilock; and so the glad tidings flew round the neighbourhood.

Everyone sang the praises of the happy couple and it was generally agreed that it was an excellent match, and Mr Lark, when he heard the news from Mrs Digby, was inspired to emulate Tom Hawley and he resolved to redouble his efforts to win the other prize Mr Allen had left to offer; and in this he was encouraged by Mrs Knox remarking, with an arch smile, that perhaps he would be the next to get married.

The fuss that was being made over Harriet was a welcome distraction to Caroline. With luck, she hoped that her unfortunate encounter with Sir James on Cullaton Moor might be forgotten. And the longer Sir James delayed telling anyone about it the more difficult he would find it to convince people he was speaking the truth, since it would be accounted rather odd of him to have waited several days before informing her guardians; at least that was how Caroline liked to reassure herself, though in her innermost heart she knew she was being just a little sanguine.

As Emberhope was to be honoured with a visit from the Bishop of Durham, who was coming for the Harvest Festival service, the Knoxs had arranged to hold a garden party for him on the day before.

They couldn't have chosen a better day, and when the Grange carriage set out for the Rectory the sun was shining brilliantly out of a serene, blue sky. Mrs Allen was a magnificent figure in a gown of purple silk and a gorgeous plumed bonnet. Harriet looked bewitching in a pretty, white muslin dress with a sash of grass green and a white silk bonnet with ribbons matching her sash, while her cousin was in primrose yellow with a sash of forget-me-not blue and a matching bonnet.

Caroline anticipated the garden party with no feelings of joy for there were two guests whom she had to avoid at all cost. In this she was successful till after tea when the guests left the tables to saunter about the ample lawn. She was talking to one of the Digby boys when they were joined by Sir James Reddaway. The modest Digby youth faded quietly away and Caroline found herself strolling down the lawn with the baronet towards a rose arch which led to another part of the garden.

"Shall we go down here for a few minutes?" he suggested, stepping aside for her to pass under the rose arch. "I find the incessant chatter fatiguing."

Since she did not want to put him out of humour, Caroline agreed with an air of languid indifference and proceeded by his side down the path.

"I have been meaning to call upon you all this week," he continued when they were out of sight of the lawn, "because I wished to assure myself that you had suffered no ill-effects from your — er — expedition the other night."

"Thank you, Sir James. It was very considerate of you," was the dispassionate response.

"I can see that you have not suffered from being out in the night air," he observed, with a smile.

G

"I am quite well, thank you, sir. I sustained no injury from being out on the moor," Caroline said, keeping her eyes on the path ahead.

"Heaven forbid that you should!" he cried. He was silent for a moment. "Are you still angry with me?"

"Angry with you, Sir James! No!"

"You were."

"Well, you were not very polite."

"I'm sorry you should have thought that. But I was concerned for your safety. After all, you were taking a great risk, you know."

"I liked it."

"No doubt. But there are some things we ought not to do however much we may like doing them."

Caroline was beginning to resent his admonitory tone. "Possibly. But as no harm has come of my going to the moor there can be no need to worry about it any longer."

"I wish I could feel sure of that."

Caroline glanced up at him in surprise. "What do you mean, sir?"

"I cannot be certain that you aren't contemplating another visit."

"Oh, you need have no fears on that account!" she laughed. "I assure you I have no intention of going again. My experience the other night was too disagreeable for me to want a repetition of it."

"There you see — you are still angry with me!" he cried.

"No, I'm not!" she denied, rather unreasonably. "But I didn't want anyone to know I'd been out alone after dark."

"No one shall."

Caroline looked up at him again but it was impossible to divine what was going on behind those grave, inscrutable features; yet she felt sure there was a purpose behind his remarks, that he was trying to catch her out.

"I'm sorry if I offended you," he went on in a placatory tone. "But you must admit you were one of the last people I should have expected to meet."

"Oh, yes."

"And the circumstances seemed at first a trifle — suspicious."

"You have no justification for saying that, sir!" she countered hotly.

"Have I not?"

Her eyes met his briefly; but except for a ghost of a smile his face remained an unfathomable mask and she could not tell whether he was bluffing or whether he really did know the truth. "The same might be said of yourself, sir," she retorted.

He threw back his head and uttered a gay laugh. "True! I may be one of his accomplices — or even the Midnight Horseman himself!" he joked genially.

But Caroline wasn't going to be deceived by his jocularity, and sensing a trap behind his remark, she replied warily "That is a possibility."

He regarded her with amusement. "Now we are letting our imaginations get the better of us."

"You have done the same, Sir James."

"Yes, yes, I agree," he laughed. "But don't let's quarrel. I don't want to make you angry."

"Then be good enough not make any more ridiculous insinuations, sir," Caroline said, with aggressive bluntness. "You can hardly expect me to like being told my behaviour was suspicious."

Her bold attitude evidently impressed him and he made haste to mollify her. "Let us say no more about the affair," he said. "I own I was in the wrong and should not have said what I did, and I offer you my most humble apologies while withdrawing unconditionally all I have said." He peeped round the corner of her bonnet. "Am I forgiven?"

"Yes," she answered, but without looking at him.

"I haven't given up hope that I may yet be considered worthy of you," he went on in a more serious vein, "and I shall strive to convince you by my constancy of the sincerity of my affections and the steadfastness of my devotion to you."

They had turned back by now and Caroline deliberately refrained from saying anything for a few moments since they would shortly be back on the lawn. "I should prefer you not to persevere, sir, for I can promise you no hope of success," she murmured, quickening her pace.

"I wish I knew why," he sighed. "Tell me — is there some defect in my character of which you disapprove? Have you reason to think ill of my temper?" he questioned earnestly.

Caroline recollected that she had judged him to be a man of uncertain temper, but she had no intention of admitting it since it would invite further discussion, which was the last thing she wanted. "No, sir, I do not think ill of you in any respect." The rose arch was in sight at last. "Hadn't we better rejoin the others, Sir James? They will think us uncivil if we stay away too long." A few rapid steps and she was through the rose arch and back on the lawn again.

But her trials were not over yet. Their absence had not gone unnoticed by their hostess and when Caroline walked on to the lawn Mrs Knox came across to her. "Caroline, my dear, I want you to come and talk to the bishop. He is most anxious to make your acquaintance," she explained, with a winning smile.

"The bishop!" Caroline echoed in an astonished tone; then recollecting herself. "Oh, yes — by all means!"

She followed Mrs Knox docilely across the grass to where the bishop was standing amongst a group of clergymen.

"So this is the young lady!" he said, with a smiling glance at Mr Lark who was standing at his elbow, his figure bent in a deferential curve. "I am delighted to make your acquaintance, my child. I have heard a great deal about you and I am sure it is well merited."

"Thank you, my lord," Caroline answered, lowering her eyes modestly.

"You live at Ullingham Grange, I believe?" inquired his lordship.

"Yes, my lord."

"You are fond of Northumberland?"

"Yes, very."

"You have no desire to live in another county?"

"I do not think so, my lord."

"Splendid! Splendid! It would be a great pity if we were to be robbed of such a charming and talented, young lady — eh, Archdeacon?"

The archdeacon bowed his concurrence and the bishop smiled benevolently at Caroline. "And now that your cousin is to be married we must ensure that we do not lose you by seeing you safely settled in a home of your own too. Yes, to be sure, that is what we must do!"

The old gentleman beamed in great good-humour at his little joke, in which all joined except Caroline who stood with downcast eyes, striving to stem the tide of resentment rising within her as she realised that the bishop's aid had been enlisted to induce her to marry Mr Lark.

"I think I am too young yet to make a very good wife," she objected mildly.

"Too young! Nonsense, my dear!" the bishop contradicted good-naturedly. "Endowed as you undoubtedly are with an engaging and vivacious disposition and a refined and informed mind you would be not only an amiable partner to a young man at the outset of his career but an asset of immeasurable worth."

"You are very kind, my lord. I hope I shall not disappoint your expectations of me," was the sedate response.

"I have not the slightest fear of that," he assured her paternally. "I am confident that you will make an admirable wife."

Caroline acknowledged these well-intentioned compliments with a sweet smile; and as a number of guests were hovering on the fringe of the little group, waiting to take their leave, she was permitted to retire; and shortly afterwards she, too, left the Rectory with her aunt and uncle. It cannot be said that the bishop's little homily had kindled in her heart a spirit of compliance and goodwill; nor had it improved Mr Lark's prospects. Caroline's mind was now absolutely resolved upon one thing, that the man she married should be of her own free choice and she was not going to tolerate any interference in this vital matter.

Mr Allen, who was sitting opposite her in the carriage, noticed her compressed lips and peevish, little frown and wondered what had occurred to put her out of temper. But being unaware of the plans that were being made for his niece's future, the Squire of Ullingham Grange had not yet discovered how greatly his help was needed.

Chapter Twelve

One afternoon during the following week, when Mrs Allen had taken Harriet to Emberhope to do some shopping, Caroline was curled upon the settee in the drawing room with a novel on her knees. She was so engrossed in her book that she did not notice that her uncle was standing at the door, regarding her thoughtfully.

His good-natured face wore a harassed look as he began to move with hesitant steps across the room. "Caroline — "

On hearing his gentle voice, Caroline looked up from her book with a little gasp. "Oh — how you startled me, Uncle George! I didn't know there was anyone in the room!"

"I beg your pardon, my dear," her uncle apologised meekly. "I have only just come in and you were so deep in your book you didn't hear me. Er — is it a good tale?"

"Yes — very," Caroline answered, smiling up at him.

"Then my intrusion is most ill-timed," he said, with a kindly smile, "and I hope you will forgive me."

"Why — of course, Uncle George! I can continue it later!" Caroline exclaimed, putting the book down beside her.

"Er — yes — quite so." Mr Allen fidgeted about, clearly ill-at-ease, while Caroline watched him perplexedly. "My dear — " he essayed again nervously. "I wonder — can you spare me a moment? But there is a matter of some importance I must speak to you about."

Caroline's heart missed a beat and she looked away to hide her guilty flush. There could be only one thing he could mean for his hesitant manner suggested that what he had to say was distasteful to him.

"Certainly, Uncle . . ." Her voice faded away into inaudibility.

"Well — er — the fact is — I mean — " The shufflings of his feet and the incoherence of his speech indicated that Mr Allen was no less uneasy than his niece. "I have had a visitor this afternoon — he was quite unexpected — my dear, it was Sir James Reddaway!"

The last sentence came out with a rush and Caroline, who had turned and stared at him anxiously as he struggled for words, stiffened visibly for her worst fears seemed about to be confirmed. She lowered her head and waited in miserable suspense for him to continue.

"He came to — well, I think you may conjecture the reason for his visit," he ventured, hoping that she would come to his aid.

"Yes — I mean — no — " Caroline answered confusedly. "No, Uncle George!"

Mr Allen was greatly put out by this response and he took a turn up and down the room before going on again. "My dear, I don't quite know how to begin," he said, halting at last on the hearth rug, "for it is rather a delicate subject for me to speak about." He paused awkwardly. "But let me go straight to the heart of the matter. My dear, Sir James begs leave to make you a proposal of marriage!" He looked anxiously at his niece to see what effect this announcement had on her, but seeing her still with downcast eyes which he construed as bashfulness, he continued "Believing that you were held back from returning his good opinion by uncertainty as to whether such an attachment would meet with the approval of your aunt and myself, he has come this afternoon to ascertain my views and to ask me to remove any doubts that may exist in your mind by giving my sanction to the attachment. I admit I was much taken aback at first as I was unaware of there ever having been anything between you two. But then Sir James assured me that he had received sufficient encouragement to give him good reason to hope for success — " The look of indignation which crossed his niece's face escaped his notice. " — I could not reasonably withhold my consent, and I told him I would willingly agree to his paying his addresses to you though, of course, I could not speak with any knowledge of your feelings." Mr Allen regarded his niece's bowed head anxiously while he waited for her to speak.

She looked up and in a halting voice asked "Is — is that — all he wished to speak to you about?"

"Why — yes, my dear! Our interview was brief for immediately I had given him my answer Sir James said he would like to see you. He is waiting now in the library."

Mr Allen was much mistaken if he thought this information would be received with pleasure. Caroline jumped up from the settee in great consternation. "Oh, no, not yet, Uncle George!" she cried in an urgent tone. "Please don't let him come in yet! I can't see him now!"

Sir James's application had taken Mr Allen by surprise, but the baronet had been so insistent and so confident that he was satisfied that his niece could have no serious objection to the proposal. Her response, therefore, was somewhat disconcerting. But thinking diffidence was perhaps the cause of her agitation, he said "Of course, my dear, I understand how you feel. You must have a little time to think things over and your caution does you credit." He patted her arm kindly. "But, Caroline, we must not keep the gentleman waiting too long. That would be unkind," he reminded her gently.

"You do not understand," she murmured, turning from him. She faced him again and said in a firm voice "Uncle George, it is not true that I gave him encouragement — quite the reverse. I have refused him!"

Poor Mr Allen! This unexpected turn of events left him dumbfounded. Here was a highly eligible suitor for his niece's hand who was clearly very much in love with her and she would not have him — had, in fact, rejected an offer from him already! "*Refused him!*" he gasped weakly.

"Yes."

"But — I don't understand! You like him, don't you?"

"Yes, but no more than any other gentleman of my acquaintance."

Mr Allen, at a loss for words and very disturbed, began to pace between the door and the hearth rug. "It is strange — very strange!" he muttered unhappily. "Sir James seemed so certain!" He stopped by the fireplace. "My child, are you certain you have given the matter fair consideration?"

"Yes, yes!" she cried vehemently. "He proposed to me more than a week ago and I haven't changed my mind!"

It was beginning to dawn on Mr Allen that a great deal had been going on unbeknownst to him. "It is beyond my comprehension!" he exclaimed. "Here is a gentleman much respected in the county, blessed with an ample fortune, by no means unhandsome, with a steady character and an amiable and considerate disposition. Caroline, are you sure you are not being too hasty?" he persisted in an earnest manner.

Caroline shook her head despairingly. "I know it is difficult for you to understand, Uncle George," she sighed. "But I'm sure I'm right in refusing him. I have never been the least bit in love with him and — oh, 'tis not true that I have encouraged him!" she wailed in vexation. "He has no right to say that!"

Mr Allen could do no more. He realised that it would be of no avail to try to persuade Caroline to change her mind, nor would his conscience let him risk driving her into marriage against her inclination. But he was worried, very worried, for he was also well aware that Sir James had a strong will too and would not easily forgive this lamentable affair which must inevitably give rise to some ill-feeling. And in spite of Caroline's denial he could not bring himself to believe that Sir James had misled him about receiving encouragement from her. "Well, my dear, you must tell him so yourself. He is so confident of success that it will be useless for me to try to show him he is mistaken," he said, going towards the door. "Ah dear, 'tis all most unfortunate!" he murmured to himself, shaking his head dolefully. "I do not like it at all! No, I do not!"

He walked slowly out of the room, leaving Caroline gazing after him as if in a trance. Recollecting herself, she went over to the window where she stood looking out into the garden, her mind weighed down with the gloomiest thoughts. The weather was deteriorating gradually, almost as if in sympathy with her unhappiness. Dark, threatening thunderclouds were gathering blackly on the distant skyline and the air had become very still; not a flower, not a leaf stirring in the quiet garden, and the birds, frightened by the approaching storm, were silent in the tree tops.

All at once she sensed that there was someone in the room with her. She glanced over her shoulder and then spun round with a scared, little cry. Sir James Reddaway was standing just behind her. "I beg your pardon. Did I frighten you?" he said, with an apologetic smile.

"Y-es, a little," she admitted, with a catch in her voice, shrinking defensively against the window seat. "I thought I was alone."

"I apologise most sincerely!" he said. "But I had to come in and see you." He paused; then he said simply "I am going away."

"Going away!" Caroline repeated dully; recovering her wits, she asked "Will you be away long?"

He shrugged. "Perhaps. I don't know." He waved his hand to the settee. "Won't you sit down?"

The gilt clock on the mantelpiece told Caroline that her aunt and Harriet would not be home for at least half an hour; and she endeavoured to simulate an air of unconcern as she walked to the settee, though her knees were weak beneath her and her heart was beating furiously.

"Your uncle gave me your message," Sir James continued, dropping down on to the other end of the settee. "Is that to be your final, irrevocable answer?"

There seemed to be an ominously challenging ring about this question but she replied calmly "Yes, sir."

"But why? Oh, Caroline, I love you dearly! You are everything to me! You will break my heart if you reject me!" He leant towards her and she drew back quickly. "Dearest one, have I no place at all in your affections?"

Caroline was finding it extremely difficult to remain composed in the face of such ardent love-making. He had taken her hands in his, and as he pressed his face closer to hers she felt she was being carried away by the strong tide of his passion and she was terrified lest he should suddenly seize her in his arms for she doubted whether she would be able to resist him then. "I — esteem your friendship highly, sir, but I — cannot — love you," she stammered. "I beg of you not to be so persistent. It distresses me — "

"No, no, don't say that!" he broke in, in a tone of anguish. "I wouldn't distress you for the world! But don't reject me so hastily, I implore you! Think — think what happiness we could enjoy together! Everything I possess shall be directed for your benefit if you will but make me the happiest and proudest of men by becoming my wife!"

"I can do no more than thank you most sincerely, sir, she replied, struggling to withdraw her hands. "I am deeply sensible of the great compliment you have paid me but — I cannot marry you."

She looked up at him fearfully, wondering what he would do. His dark eyes, glowing with a strangely terrifying light which reflected the power of his wild passion, peered searchingly into hers for a few moments.

Then he released her hands and stood up. "You really — mean that?"

"Yes. Oh, I don't want to hurt you!" she burst out, her voice sounding almost pathetic in its sincerity. "But surely you must see it's no use pretending!"

"No, I suppose not," he acknowledged, with a heavy sigh, walking away from her. He made a gesture of hopelessness and stood with his head sunk moodily on his chest; then he looked up. "I will leave you." Just as he seemed to be about to leave her without a word of farewell he paused with his hand on the door knob; then he returned a few steps. "I nearly forgot — I haven't told you of the discovery there has been made in connection with the murder. I think it will interest you."

Caroline looked away quickly to prevent his seeing the alarm which she knew her eyes must betray.

"Some property belonging to the dead man and the weapon with which he was probably killed have been found," Sir James went on. He saw her shudder and he said evenly "They will help us considerably in our efforts to trace the murderer and bring him to the judgment he deserves — the gallows."

"Oh, no, don't speak of that! 'Tis horrible!" she protested, putting her hands over her ears in distress.

"It was a horrible crime and one which cannot go unpunished," he rejoined sternly, "and the magistrates are agreed that no effort must be spared to apprehend the murderer."

"Have you any suspicions as to the identity of the murderer?" She repented her folly as soon as she had spoken, yet she had been unable to resist the urge to ask the question.

"Need you ask?" he replied in a soft voice which sent a thrill of fear through her.

"No, I suppose not."

"Who else could it possibly be but that highwayman?"

"Can you prove that it was he?"

His eyes half closed in the suspicion of a smile. "It would seem that I have awakened your interest," he commented drily.

"'Tis hardly surprising considering how much it interests everyone else."

"Then let me trespass on your time a little longer to tell you something else. The articles I mentioned just now in themselves are of little value to us. But two nights ago this man was seen leaving the house where the missing property and the knife were found." He waited to see if she would say anything but she sat staring fixedly before her. "You do not speak. Have you no opinion to offer?"

"My poor opinion can scarcely be of value to such as yourself who have so much greater understanding of these matters," she answered.

With an abruptness which took her unawares, he leant forward and whispered "But we have not your — knowledge!"

"My knowledge!" she repeated in astonishment. "What do you mean, Sir James. I have no knowledge that can be of use to you!"

His expression relented as he sat down beside her again and said gently "Why are you being so foolish, Caroline? Why do you persist in denying what you know is the truth? It's useless for you to pretend you aren't hiding something when your whole manner declares that you have a secret which you don't want anyone to know."

"I have no secrets of which I need be ashamed!" she retorted.

"Can you shield a murderer and remain unashamed?" he challenged swiftly.

"I am not shielding a murderer!"

"Then whom were you with the other night?"

She rounded on him, her eyes flashing angrily. "Sir James, I will not endure it! I refuse to submit to another cross-examination! Haven't you insulted me enough already with your questions?"

He stood up and she could see that the gentleness had gone from his face and there was a dour, pitiless hardness in his eyes. "You would prefer, then, to be cross-examined before one of His Majesty's Judges of Assize?"

She fought desperately to overcome the panic which surged up within her, urging her to acknowledge the truth and end the whole agonising torment. Oh, if only she knew whether he was just trying to trick her by bluffing or whether he really had found out what she had been doing on Cullaton Moor! "What do you mean?" she demanded in rapid tones.

"Simply this. The house I have just told you about was the one in which I found you last Tuesday night."

An icy chill closed round her heart and a sudden faintness seized her, making the room swim dizzily before her eyes, and she dug her fingers into the edge of the settee in a superhuman effort to retain her fast dwindling self-control. "I don't see what that has to do with me," she maintained.

"Don't you think your presence in that place requires an explanation," he pointed out, studying her face with watchful eyes. "Your being on Cullaton Moor was harmless enough, I grant you; but what took you to that hovel? Not mere curiosity." He shook his head. "No, your purpose lay deeper than that," he challenged accusingly. "You had an assignation, hadn't you?" He had won and he knew it as he looked down, with a smile of triumph, at her bowed head and he knelt down beside her. "Caroline, my darling, is it necessary to risk so much for such a worthless creature?" he reasoned gently.

"He isn't worthless!" she denied in a fierce whisper.

"Then you have met him!" he cried, jumping to his feet. "Caroline, I insist upon an answer! You have met the Midnight Horseman, haven't you?"

Browbeaten by his remorseless questioning, she gave in. "Yes, I have met him," she agreed wearily.

"Caroline! Do you comprehend what you are saying?" he gasped, drawing back from her aghast. "Do you realise the gravity of your admission?"

"Yes, I realise," she answered in a choking voice. "You may do what you like now. I don't care."

"Oh, good God, I can't bear it!" he burst out frenziedly, clapping his hand to his brow. "Caroline, I implore you not to be carried away by this mad caprice! Tell me all you know about this man so that I can save your name before it's too late!" He came and sat down beside her. "My dearest girl, I beseech you to pause an instant and think what you are about. You know that no one has a greater interest in your welfare than I. If what I have said has offended you, remember it is because I love you dearly. It would break my heart if anything were to happen to you. Oh, my darling, please, please let me help you!" he pleaded urgently. "Only confide in me and I swear to you that your secret shall go no further!"

"No, sir, I don't want your help," she answered doggedly, getting up and walking away from him. "The best thing you can do now is to leave me," she said, keeping her back turned.

He did not move for a moment or two, but sat glaring at her back, his hands clenched, his lips compressed in an ugly, vicious line. Then he got slowly to his feet and there was an edge to his voice as he said "I think I understand now. You're not helping him because you pity him but because — " his voice changed to a sneer, " — you've fallen in love with him."

Her eyes blazed as she turned on him, her face pale, her hands gripped tightly at her sides. "Go away! Go away!" she commanded in a voice vibrant with anger. "I won't answer any more of your horrible questions! I hate you and I never want to see you again!" She turned her back on him again and there was a deathly silence in the room.

At length he spoke, his voice sounding to her as if from afar off. "Very well, I can do no more. You have only yourself to blame now." He strolled into the middle of the room. "So you're in love with a highwayman!" he jeered.

Caroline was by now so overwrought, her nerves strained to breaking point by their battle of wits, that she was past caring what she said or did; and stung by this final taunt, she flung round in a passion. "Well, what if I am?" she demanded furiously.

"Oh, nothing," he returned, with a contemptuous shrug. "Except that in a little while all you'll have left to love will be a corpse dangling on the end of a gibbet rope."

They stood facing each other, he cold and sardonic, she trembling with the wild ferment of fury which stormed within her.

Then, fearlessly, she crossed the room to him with short, quick steps. "You devil! You cold-blooded, inhuman devil!" she whispered, biting viciously on each word. "How dare you speak to me like that!"

Save for a slight, derisive smile which enraged her still more he remained unmoved by this onslaught. "There are none so blind as they that will not see," he mocked, though with a bitterness that betrayed his deep mortification. "What a pretty picture you'll present kneeling in tears at the foot of the gibbet! So touching! So — "

He got no further. Caroline's last vestiges of self-control deserted her as she listened to his sneering, drawling voice. "You beast!" As she hissed the words out at him she raised her hand and slapped his face with all her strength.

He staggered back, unable for the moment to believe his senses; but recovering himself, he lurched towards her, his flushed features distorted in a fiendish snarl and raised his arms as if he would seize her. But recalling where he was, he checked himself and let his arms drop to his sides. "It is clear that you are beyond the reach of reason," he said icily.

"If you insist on being so wilful you must bear the consequences of your actions alone. I shall not burden you with my presence any longer." He turned on his heel and strode to the door.

Just as he was about to open it Caroline spoke. "Sir James — "

He stopped but did not turn round. "Yes?"

"What . . . are you going to do?"

"I am going to see that every effort is made to capture the Midnight Horseman and, if necessary, any accomplices he may have. I bid you a very good day."

Dimly she heard the faint click of the door as it closed behind him, but her thoughts were already far beyond the walls of the room and she stared unseeingly at the cream panels of the door, stunned by this frightful disaster. Then, as her numbed senses took in the full significance of the situation, she collapsed limply against the window seat.

Oh, good heavens, what had she done? Betrayed him to his pursuers when she had promised him faithfully not to give him away! Now what would he think of her? She who had begged to be allowed to help him was now to be his greatest source of danger — oh, the irony of it! Fool, fool! She flung her head down on the window seat and her small shoulders shook convulsively as the hot, bitter tears poured forth.

After a while her passionate sobs began to weaken, and raising her head, she rubbed her sleeve across her tear-stained face and got up. Oh, why was she being so silly, she asked herself crossly? Sir James was quite right; she was letting herself be carried away by a mad caprice. She sniffed tearfully and gazed out of the window. Yet she couldn't bear the thought of anything happening to him. No, no, they mustn't catch him! But what could she do to help him? She wrung her hands in an agony of distraction as she realised that there was no way in which she could get in touch with him. Oh, she wished she'd never met him! The unhappiness and disgrace she would bring on her own family too — it would have been better if she had accepted Sir James and surrendered to a life of loveless, affluent respectability! She shuddered involuntarily. No, that was unthinkable after the infamous way he had treated her! However much she had wounded his feelings by rejecting him he had no right to avenge himself like that!

She was aroused from her unhappy meditations by a door banging in the hall and she spun round with a guilty start as Harriet burst into the room. "Caroline, has Sir James Reddaway been to see you?" she demanded excitedly.

"Yes."

"I thought he had," Harriet chattered on breathlessly. "We met him at the bend in the road and when Mama ordered Vince to stop so that she could speak to him he asked if he might have a few words in private with her and she made me get down and walk the rest of the way." She paused for breath and then asked "Did he stay long?"

"No, not very," Caroline answered, turning away.

"What did he want?"

"Nothing in particular."

Harriet regarded her cousin's back curiously. "But he came to see you, didn't he?" she pursued.

"Yes."

The furtiveness of her cousin's manner did not tend to quieten Harriet's curiosity and a puzzled frown clouded her face. "Was it as secret as all that?" she said.

"There wasn't anything secret about him calling. He saw Uncle George first," Caroline said dully.

There was an uncomfortable silence, till Harriet said "I can't make you out, Caroline. You've been so quiet these last few days. Why won't you tell me what he came for? You don't usually hide anything from me," she added reproachfully.

"There isn't anything to tell!" Caroline exclaimed querulously, turning to her. "Oh, do leave me alone, Harriet! I don't want to talk about him!"

"Oh, all right, you needn't tell me if you don't wish to!" Harriet returned huffily. "I'm sure I've no desire to pry into your affairs!" She sat down on the settee and began to untie the ribbons of her bonnet.

Caroline glanced at her in dismay, and seeing her disgruntled, little scowl, she ran over to her. "Please don't be cross with me, Harriet!" she begged, kneeling down beside her cousin. "I couldn't bear you to be unkind to me too!"

Harriet looked down in amazement at the grey eyes which were brimming with tears. "Caroline, whatever's the matter?" she cried, putting her arms round her. "Why — you're trembling!"

"Oh, Harriet, I'm so miserable! I know 'tis all my own fault but — Sir James was horrid to me!" Caroline sobbed, burying her face in Harriet's lap.

"Sir James horrid to you! But, dearest, he's in love with you!"

"I know, I know I wish he wasn't!" Caroline wailed. "Oh, why won't he leave me alone!"

She broke into renewed sobs and Harriet sat looking down at her, too nonplussed by her extraordinary behaviour to know what to say. "Caroline . . . has he . . . asked you to . . . marry him?" she asked very tentatively.

"Y-es!"

Harriet was defeated. She gazed helplessly round the room and then said "But, Caroline, there's no need to be upset! No one will be angry with you for refusing him if you don't love him!"

"But you — don't understand!" Caroline gulped out between sobs. "Oh, how I hate him! He's an odious creature!"

She wept unrestrainedly and Harriet put her arms round her to try to comfort her. "Please don't cry, Caroline!" she urged. "It will be all right — I'm sure it will!" She glanced up suddenly, a look of alarm on her face. "Oh dear! Here's Mama!" She pushed Caroline's head in consternation. "Caroline, do stop crying before she comes in!" she besought her, pulling out her handkerchief and mopping her cousin's moist cheeks in frenzied haste.

The next moment the door was flung open and the two girls sprang apart as Mrs Allen swept into the drawing room. At the sight of the fiery glint in her eyes Harriet darted to the far side of the room, leaving Caroline standing by the fireplace with her back turned, hastily dabbing her eyes.

"Caroline, what is this monstrous story I have just heard from Sir James?" Mrs Allen began in a tone which boded ill for her niece. "He tells me he found you out alone on Cullaton Moor last Tuesday night! Is this true?" Upon receiving no immediate answer she banged her parasol impatiently on the carpet. "Answer me this instant! Is it true what he says?"

"Y-es, Aunt Julia."

"Caroline, how dared you! You must have been insane!" Mrs Allen exclaimed, horrified by this admission. "What were you doing there?" she demanded. "Don't stand with your back to me like that!" she raged, stamping her foot angrily. "I insist upon knowing everything!"

Caroline turned slowly round, her eyes downcast. "I've nothing to tell you," she muttered sulkily.

"Insolent girl — I shall not be denied an answer!" her aunt cried, striding up to her in a fury. "What were you doing out on the moor?"

"I wanted to see the Midnight Horseman."

"Caroline! Have you no self-respect! Have you no shame!" Mrs Allen's voice sank to an appalled whisper. "Is this how your uncle and I are to be repaid for our trouble? To have you wandering about Cullaton Moor like a — a — " She could not bring herself to say the word. "Oh, it is too frightful!" she moaned. "And am I to understand that you have actually met this man?"

"Hasn't Sir James told you everything?" was the sullen reply.

"He told me he suspected you to be in possession of information which will assist in tracing this man." Caroline turned away and covered her face with her hands, which only infuriated her aunt the more. "Caroline, I intend to know the whole truth of this matter. Tell me at once what secrets you are hiding?"

"No, no, I won't!" Caroline cried wildly, bursting into tears.

"Oh, you wicked girl!" exclaimed her aunt in great exasperation. "How dare you defy me! You deserve a good whipping! But I shall not be put off! I shall know the truth! Tell me — have you met the Midnight Horseman?"

"Yes, I have — twice!" Caroline flung at her in tempestuous defiance.

"Twice! *Twice!*" Mrs Allen shrieked. "Oh, what will people think! All our friends — the Knoxs — the Digbys — Lady Heston-ffolliott! And Mr Lark too! Do you think he'll want to marry you now!"

"I don't care what he thinks! He's a silly, pompous, conceited idiot and I won't marry him however hard you try to make me — no, not even if you whip me and starve me and — "

"Stop it! Stop it!" broke in her aunt furiously. "I shall not be spoken to in this way! You are a self-willed, unprincipled girl and you shall be severely punished!" Mrs Allen gave herself time to recover her breath. "Go to your room and remain there till you are sent for!" she commanded sternly. "I shall speak to your uncle immediately so that he may decide how to deal with you!"

Caroline needed no second bidding. With her hands over her face, sobbing heartbrokenly, she ran out of the room and stumbled blindly upstairs to her bedroom.

"Harriet, be good enough to fetch your father," Mrs Allen requested, sitting down in her chair with as much dignity as her hot and angry countenance would permit.

Harriet scurried out of the room like a frightened rabbit but returned shortly to say that her father was not in. When Sir James had left Caroline he had walked straight out of the house, and Mr Allen only heard of his departure from his butler some minutes after he had gone. As he had wanted to go and inspect a field that was being harvested Mr Allen had gone out without looking into the drawing room to see how Sir James had fared in his love-making; to tell the truth, he had been afraid to.

So Mrs Allen was forced to defer her consultation with her husband till later, which did not soothe her, since she was seething with impatience to discuss her niece's misdemeanours; and when Harriet generously, but unwisely, attempted to plead on Caroline's behalf she only turned Mrs Allen's wrath in her own direction. In trying to explain that her cousin's intention had merely been to go and watch for the Midnight Horseman she unfortunately showed that she had been in Caroline's confidence in the first place. She was promptly subjected to a searching interrogation as to her part in the affair; and though she was able to satisfy her mother that she had not played an active role she did not escape a severe scolding. She was an ungrateful, deceitful girl and her conduct was quite unpardonable, and the definitely one-sided conversation ended with the future Mrs Hawley of Mellaton being dismissed to her room like a naughty child, whither she retired, humiliated and in tears, somewhat to the dismay of Mr Allen who, happening to be crossing the hall at that moment, nearly collided with his daughter as she rushed out of the drawing room.

"Harriet seems upset," he said in the mildest of voices as he went in. "Is anything wrong, my dear?" He regretted his question as soon as he saw his wife's face.

"Wrong! Yes, there is a great deal wrong!" Mrs Allen answered grimly; and without more ado she retailed to him all that had happened.

"No, it's impossible! There must be some mistake — or, at least, some explanation!" he argued, with unusual energy, when he was at last permitted to speak.

"Very well, ask Caroline yourself. Ask her for an explanation. I have questioned her and she was insolent, grossly insolent! You must deal with her now. Send for her at once and demand to know the truth."

That Mr Allen anticipated another interview with his niece with little joy was only too evident from his glum expression as he pulled the bell cord.

"You must be firm with her, George," Mrs Allen warned him. "On no account must you let yourself be deceived by her. She is a wicked, headstrong girl and must be made to divulge her secrets."

"I shall do my best, my dear," he promised, without much conviction. "Oh, Bertram," he said to the butler who was waiting in the doorway, "ask Miss Caroline to come down to the library."

"Miss Caroline has just gone out, sir."

"Gone out! Are you sure of it, Bertram?" demanded Mrs Allen.

"Yes, ma'am. A child from Knapmans asked to speak to her and she went out into the road with him."

Mrs Allen's expression was charged with meaning as she looked at her husband.

"Very well, Bertram, it will do later," he said hastily, waving the butler away.

"And now, George, what do you intend to do?" Mrs Allen said. "Caroline has left the house in direct defiance of my orders."

"I can do nothing till she returns, Julia," he replied, retreating towards the door. "Unless — " He pondered a moment. "Perhaps it would be as well if I locked Harriet up."

He did not wait to hear his wife's views on this suggestion.

Chapter Thirteen

In the quieter atmosphere of her bedroom Caroline's passionate feelings subsided quickly and she began to regret her outburst, realising that her hot-headed behaviour had only made matters worse. And when the housemaid came to tell her that little Willy Knapman was asking for her, reminded of her aunt's edict, she at first said she could not come; but then, feeling it would be a relief to get some fresh air, she called the maid back and told her she would see the child.

Putting on her bonnet, she crept secretly down the back stairs and out of the house to the stable gate where she found the little boy waiting for her.

When she asked him what he wanted he mumbled something about "Miss was wanted up the road" and beckoned vigorously in that direction. Thinking something was wrong at the Knapmans' farm, Caroline agreed to go with him.

As she followed the lad up the road towards Cullaton Moor a carriage drew up beside her and a man put his head out of the window and inquired of her the way to Hexham. She turned and pointed ahead.

What happened next she never really quite knew. A horny hand was clapped over her mouth and she was swung off her feet and thrown roughly inside the carriage which set off instantly at a brisk pace. To forestall any resistance she might attempt a coarse woollen scarf was thrust into her mouth and a rug was wrapped tightly round her body. Pressed down into the seat, Caroline could see no more than the broad backs of two burly men on either side of her.

They had travelled several miles when the carriage began to slacken speed. Its wheels scrunched harshly in the dust as it lurched ponderously round a bend and then it went on, jolting and swaying, at a more cautious rate down a rutty lane till it halted at last under some trees which brushed against its roof. The rug was thrown across Caroline's face and she was lifted out of the carriage and carried some little distance and up a flight of stairs where she was dumped on the ground and the rug was taken off her; before she could get even a glimpse of them her captors had left her.

Her bewildered eyes blinked dazedly as she surveyed her surroundings. She was in a long garret in the eaves of the roof, with yellow, damp-stained walls and a steep, sloping ceiling reaching almost to the floor on either side. In one wall there was a square lattice window, but as it was built out from the roof it did little more than light up the part of the room opposite its deep sill. In the middle of the floor there were a couple of rickety chairs and a small, round table and in the corner furthest from the door an old linen chest. The huge, grey cobwebs hanging in the corners of the rafters and festooning the windowpanes and the layer of dust covering the worn and uneven floorboards indicated that the place had been uninhabited for a long time.

For some minutes Caroline remained staring blankly about her, too stupefied to move. Then passing her hand wearily across her eyes, she sank limply on to a chair. Whatever was all this about? Who could have wanted to abduct her? Instantly one name sprang to her mind. The Midnight Horseman! Was he, then, really the monster he was made out to be? Had he, knowing there was no other way he could posses her, sent two of his accomplices to kidnap her? She shook her head, refusing to admit this explanation. He would never stoop to such infamy.

She sat for a while deep in thought. Then all at once a possibility occurred to her and she sprang to her feet in consternation. When she had asked to be allowed to help him, she remembered he had told her that he could not risk her falling into the hands of his adversaries. Was that what had happened? Had she been brought here because his enemies thought she could be used in some way to overcome him, perhaps by extracting information from her? If that was so, then she must discover somehow a means of escaping from this house as soon as possible.

Inspired with this object, she started to examine the garret. But it did not take her long to find out that, decayed and worm-eaten though her prison was, it was too strong for her to break out of. The door was securely bolted, and as she leant across the windowsill and tried to push up the latch, rusted and stiff from disuse, she realised that even if she did succeed in opening the window it would be hopeless to attempt to escape that way since she would have to risk a drop of a considerable distance.

She peered through the smeary panes in an effort to gain some inkling of her whereabouts, but she could see little beyond the moss-lined cobbles of the yard below and the branches of the trees surrounding the house, though the steady thrash of water over a weir told her that there was a river nearby.

She drew back from the window and sank down dispiritedly on to a chair. There seemed nothing she could do but wait and see what happened in the hope that later an opportunity might offer itself. She had no means of telling the time but she judged from the declining daylight that filtered in through the window that it was early evening. The storm clouds which had been gathering in the sky all afternoon hung overhead, black and lowering, and a white flash of lightning, followed a few seconds later by a distant rumble of thunder, foretold the imminent breaking of the storm. Except for an occasional nervous rustle among the branches of the trees the air was terrifyingly still, and a strange, brooding silence hung over the old house.

Cold and hungry, her mind racked with fear, Caroline sat with her hands hanging forlornly in her lap, wondering how much longer she was going to have to endure the awful suspense. Around her, as the twilight deepened outside, a dismal murkiness settled and the outlines of the room faded into a shadowy gloom. The peals of thunder grew louder and more frequent and followed more closely upon the flashes of lightning. The black clouds hung poised overhead, awaiting their moment, and a few heavy drops of rain splashed noisily on the windowledge.

Then, with a deafening, terrifying crash of thunder, the storm broke. The rain streamed down in drenching torrents, hissing through the trees and rattling furiously on the windowpanes. Tremendous thunderclaps, which seemed to split the heavens open as they crashed overhead and rolled echoing away into the distance, shook the derelict building with such violence that it trembled to its very foundations; and the lightning, which at first had been but a few elusive flashes, now whipped across the garret in dazzling, breathtaking explosions of whiteness, tearing relentlessly into every crack and corner.

To Caroline, sitting huddled against the table, with her arm across her face as she vainly tried to shield her eyes from the blinding flashes of lightning, it seemed that the storm would never spend itself. Alone in the miserable garret with nothing to do, she felt as though she was out in the very heart of it. The rain driving against the window, the thunder, the lightning, all seemed to crowd upon her in a wild, mad maelstrom of fury. And as the horrible nightmare dragged on her remaining reserves of vitality and fortitude deserted her, till at last, when the violence of the storm began to subside, the thunder became more distant, the lightning less frequent, she could hardly keep her dazed eyes open. Gradually her body sagged forward and then, laying her head wearily on her arms, she fell asleep across the table.

Chapter Fourteen

The storm had passed when Caroline woke some time later. The room was lit by a dim, yellow light and she blinked confusedly at the long shadows stretching weirdly across the sloping ceiling, trying to comprehend her surroundings. Then, her eyes drawn towards the centre of light, she looked across to the door. Instantly her bemused senses were aroused and her slumping body straightened with a convulsive jerk, for standing in the doorway, watching her from behind the pear-shaped flame of the candle he held in his hand, was a tall man; an icy chill stole over her and an overwhelming sense of terror gripped her as she recognised the thin, austere features of Sir James Reddaway.

His eyes did not leave her as he walked slowly across to the table. "I regret most profoundly this ungallant treatment, my dear Caroline," he began in his soft, grave voice. "I hope, however, to be able to offer you preferable accommodation shortly!"

"Sir James, what is the meaning of this? Why have I been brought here by force?" Caroline demanded hotly, though her disquieted feelings rendered her voice thin and hoarse.

"The urgency of the moment drove me to it," he answered imperturbably. "I assure you it was most repugnant to me but there was no alternative."

"How dare you, sir! It is an outrage! I shall not submit — "

He held up his hand commandingly, a dangerous glint in his dark eyes, and she stopped.

"Calm yourself, my dear child." His voice was smooth. "These angry protests won't help you. Your mettlesome spirit will get you into trouble if you don't learn to restrain it."

"But you surely don't think you can win my affections in this way?" she cried, jumping to her feet.

"It is indeed unfortunate that I should have had to resort to such means. But as you rejected my offer of marriage so impetuously you

118

left me no choice. I trust in time, however, you will come to understand me better and appreciate the strength of my affection."

"But you cannot expect to keep me your prisoner for ever!"

His eyes closed in the suspicion of a smile. "Oh, but I do, you charming creature! You see . . . tonight we leave for . . . France!"

A dry, choking sensation clutched her throat and she leant against the table for support. "For France!" she repeated in a horrified whisper.

He nodded smilingly.

"Then you — are — a spy?" she jerked out timorously, hardly daring to utter the word.

The smile vanished from his face. "Who told you? How did you — " A look of enlightenment appeared on his face. "But of course, I might have guessed! Your friend the highwayman told you! Well, you won't need to worry your pretty head about him much longer!"

Something in his voice made her look up at him, her eyes alight with fear. "What do you mean?"

"Till tonight I have been his quarry. But now the positions are reversed. He's the one who is to be trapped and you, my enchanting angel" his voice sank to a whisper, "are to be the bait!"

With wildly beating heart she stared up into the relentless eyes. "What are you plotting, Sir James? Please, I beg of you, don't harm him!"

The words poured forth in a breathless, urgent rush and a sardonic smile came upon his lips. "You show an uncommon interest in the fellow's welfare," he taunted her. "Well, I'm afraid it can't be helped. My task is all but completed and I cannot afford to risk being foiled now. Besides, I've no desire to leave any traces behind me."

"But how am I to serve your purpose?" Caroline asked, struggling to conceal her desperate anxiety.

"I have taken good care to let the whole county know of your — disappearance. This man, being a brave fellow, will, I feel sure, attempt to rescue you when he hears what has happened. To do that he must come here."

"Sir James, I implore you not to do this!" she cried. "He can do you no harm once you're in France!"

A pitying smile entered his face as he listened to her. "You're so young and guileless! You know so little of the ways of this hard world!" he murmured, with unexpected tenderness. "But, Caroline, why do you bother your head about someone of whom you know so little? I'm not a bad man because I'm a spy! Your own country has its spies too! I've no wish to harm you! If you would marry me we could be so happy together!"

"No!" she interrupted him in a fierce whisper.

"But why not? I know you don't love me now, but I will be patient in the confidence that I shall eventually earn your regard which, Heaven knows, I deserve if any man does!"

"No, no!" she repeated, turning her back on him.

"But, Caroline, you know very well you can't expect to return to your family! Your uncle couldn't possibly take you back after what has happened!" He put his hands on her shoulders and pulled her gently round. "Come, say you'll marry me," he coaxed good-humouredly. "You know it's the only course left to you. I shan't mind your lost reputation."

She did not answer him immediately but remained rigid and silent in his arms, her eyes fixed on his face in a stony stare. Then, as the full realisation of his perfidy came to her and she understood the true reason for his betrayal of her to her aunt, the fierce tempest of anger and hatred seething within her breast, took possession of her. "Let me go! I detest you!" She struck viciously at his arms, and shaking herself free from his embrace, she sprang away from him. "So that's why you gave me away!" Her voice trembled with passion. "So much for your worthless promises and your professions of love! Nothing, nothing could be more contemptible than what you have done! You made love to me knowing all the time you meant to use me for your own base purposes! And when I wouldn't yield to you you thought you could overpower me by alienating me from my family and disgracing me in the eyes of my friends! But I won't give in to you! Do what you will with me! Take me to France! But whatever you may say nothing will ever efface the memory of the cowardly trick you have played on me! You're a false-hearted, unscrupulous blackguard and I loathe the very sight of you!"

She was shaking all over and her legs were weak under her, but she faced him gamely, defying him to do his worst to her now that he had her in his power. For a few seconds he stood glaring at her, his dark eyes inflamed with a wild, fanatical light, his tall, gaunt figure towering monstrously in the shadows of the candlelit garret. Then his features twisted in a malignant snarl and he strode across the floor, his whole frame quivering with the tumult of his fury.

Instinctively Caroline flung up her arms to protect herself but he thrust them ruthlessly behind her back, sending an agonising stab of pain through her body. Untying the ribbons of her bonnet with deft fingers, he snatched it off her head and tossed it over his shoulder. She fought furiously but vainly in his powerful grip as he pulled her down on to the linen chest. Then, pinning her down, he struck her with great, brutal blows on either side of her head, and as each successive, stinging blow fell on her ears and cheeks with merciless, unsparing force her struggles became feebler and feebler, till at last, when his raging passion was satisfied, she hung limp and unresisting in his arms and he tossed her from him to fall in a crumpled, sobbing heap in the corner, stunned and terrified by the cruel violence of his savage assault, her hands pressed to her throbbing temples and her burning, smarting cheeks. A trickle of blood ran down from her bruised and broken lips as she lay helpless on the floor, sick and faint with pain.

"Perhaps that'll curb your headstrong spirit!" he ground out, panting from exertion. "Next time you show your teeth at me I'll thrash you with a horsewhip, you bad-tempered hussy!" His insane passion arose afresh. "Stand up!" he shouted, losing his self-control. "Stand up will you!"

She did not move, nor even seemed to have heard him, and he bent over her and dragged her roughly to her feet. As she swayed giddily in his arms, her tear-dimmed eyes staring in frenzied panic out of her crimson-marked face, she thought he was going to kill her. But he lifted her off her feet and carried her across the room and threw her on to one of the chairs.

By the time her piteous sobs began to subside he had cooled down a good deal, and after walking to and fro across the floors stealing covert, worried glances at her, he sat down opposite her. "I'm sorry I hurt you. I shouldn't have done that," he muttered, ashamed to look at her. "But — oh, Caroline, I can't help myself!" he cried, turning to her with wild eyes. "You are so beautiful, so fearless — you have such vitality! I can't let you go! Caroline, Caroline, pity me for the poor, weak thing that I am! You know you have me in your power!" Beseechingly his intense gaze sought her face. But she did not even raise her head, and he wrung his hands in despair and burst forth again. "It isn't true that I only want you as a decoy! I swear I brought you here because I want to marry you! Caroline, you must believe me! It was the only choice left to me!"

Caroline still showed no sign of relenting.

"Oh, God, why am I tormented like this!" he raved, beating his fists frenziedly against his temples. "I love you to distraction! I would do anything to please you! I know I've treated you badly but it was the only way I could get you away from your guardians! Don't shun me like that, my darling!" he pleaded. "Please, please give me a chance!" But she would not look at him; and seeing that his excuses and entreaties were of no avail, he got up and walked with slow, dragging steps to the door. He leant upon it, with bowed head, for some minutes; then he turned round again. "Look, I'll reconsider my decision about the Midnight Horseman. I promise you he shall come to no harm — that I shall give up any attempt to trap him on one condition, a condition which you alone can grant."

He groaned inwardly when she did not at first show any inclination to answer him. At length she looked up at him through eyes blurred with tears. "What — is your condition?" she choked out jerkily, though she little doubted what it could be.

"Your hand in marriage."

"No, no, I will not!" she exclaimed vehemently. "How can you make such a request when you know it's impossible for me to agree to it?"

He shrugged grimly, his former ruthless manner returning. "Then my plans remain unchanged." He went towards the door. "You will forgive me if I leave you while I go and ensure that the necessary preparations have been completed."

He opened the door; but just as he was about to go out Caroline raised her head. "Sir James — "

He paused on the threshold.

"If — I accept your terms how can I be sure that you will keep your promise?"

He half turned. "I shall not wait for him to come as I had intended; we shall leave immediately before he has time to get here."

She studied him intently, trying to convince herself that she could depend upon him to keep his side of the bargain. "Do you promise me on your honour that he won't be harmed."

"Certainly. Once we're out of the country I shan't care a rap for him."

There was a tense silence while she steeled herself to take the step which must seal her fate irretrievably. If she refused Sir James's terms and delayed their departure there was a faint hope that she might escape or be rescued; but it would mean also that the horseman's life might be sacrificed, if, indeed, it wasn't sacrificed in any case for she appreciated only too well the value of the baronet's promises; and she had not forgotten what he had said about leaving no traces behind him.

But heavy though the cost must be to her, it lay in her power to protect his life, a slender chance maybe, and there was clearly only one course open to her. If she risked a gamble and it failed the horseman might be murdered, before her very eyes even, and his death would be to her an eternal reproach worse than all the other miseries she would have to endure.

"I accept your terms. I will marry you on that condition," she agreed in a whisper.

His face lit up with an exultant smile as he contemplated her abject figure, bowed in the ignominy of surrender. He went over to her, and kneeling beside her, he put his hands tenderly over hers. "You make me so happy," he murmured softly. "I promise you he shall come to no harm." He kissed her cold, pale hands and gazed pleadingly up at her but she took no notice of him. "Dearest love, don't be so unforgiving!" he entreated. "I shall make you happy! It will be my one aim in life henceforward, you may depend upon it!"

Caroline rose from the chair and walked away from him. "Do not delude yourself, sir!" she said, facing him defiantly, her head held high. "I submit to you because I have no alternative. But my heart — " her voice broke and she faltered, " — shall never be yours — no, not even if you promise me all the riches in the world."

His hands clenched convulsively as he struggled to suppress his rising anger and his eyes blazed up suddenly in his haggard face. Recovering his composure, he turned to the door. "I will give orders for the carriage to be made ready," he said coldly. "If any attempt is made to stop us I need hardly warn you that you must not betray me. You must show that you are travelling of your own accord. Do you understand?"

"Yes, I understand," she agreed miserably.

He left her without another word and she stood for a minute or two listening, in a daze, to his footsteps on the stairs. Then she went slowly back to the table, and sinking dejectedly on to a chair, flung her head on the table and burst into tears.

Chapter Fifteen

"Caroline."

At the sound of the quiet voice Caroline raised her head and stared in bewilderment at the burly figure of the Midnight Horseman standing by the table; but when she recognised him she jumped to her feet in consternation. "Oh, why have you come here? You shouldn't have come!"

"I've come for you."

"No, no, you mustn't stay here! Go away quickly before they find you!"

It was his turn to look bewildered. "But, Caroline, I can't leave you here!"

"Oh, for pity's sake go now before it's too late!" she urged frantically. "They've laid a trap for you!"

"Then the sooner we leave the better," he retorted practically.

"Oh, never mind about me! I shall only be in the way! You must go without me!"

"But, Caroline — " He drew back, baffled. "Don't you want to come?" he asked in a curious tone.

She averted her gaze and shook her head.

"You really want me to leave you here?"

"Y-es."

The tremor in her whispered reply did not escape him and he put his hands on her arms and turned her round so that he could look into her face. "Then why were you crying when I came in?"

The unwavering scrutiny of those steady grey eyes was too much for her and she buried her face in his chest. "Oh, Charles, 'tis all my fault!" she sobbed.

He fondled her thick curls with a gentle touch. "There, there, don't cry. We'll be all right," he soothed her.

"But they brought me on purpose to get you here! Sir James found me on Cullaton Moor that night and forced me to confess that I'd been with you! Oh, Charles, I've betrayed you! How can you ever forgive me?" she sobbed brokenly.

The horseman looked upwards, his jaw set grimly, and drew a deep breath; then he pushed her head up and smiled at her "Come now — dry your tears. We shall escape."

She hung submissively in his strong arms while he dabbed her moist cheeks with his handkerchief.

But precious minutes had been wasted by their argument; and as he stepped back with a cheerful grin the door was flung open and they started round to find Sir James Reddaway standing in the doorway with two men behind him. The horseman's fingers closed reassuringly round Caroline's wrist and he pushed her quietly behind him as he faced the three men.

"So our friend has arrived at last!" exclaimed the baronet. Elation shone in his eyes as he sauntered into the room. "I have long been wanting to make the acquaintance of the mysterious stranger of Cullaton Moor. It is a thousand pities that I have to leave so soon." He turned to Caroline. "I am ready, Caroline."

"She won't be going with you, Sir James," the horseman replied.

The baronet's eyebrows lifted slightly and a patient smile crossed his face. "Oh, but I think she is, my dear sir," he said, his tone suave. "You are not aware, perhaps, that she is going of her own free will."

"I am not."

"Then I suggest that you ask her yourself whether she wishes to come with me."

His assurance confounded the horseman and he turned to Caroline. "Caroline, is this true?"

She nodded her head dumbly.

"But you realise what sort of a man he is, don't you?"

"Oh, please don't argue!" she urged. "It's for the best!"

"You honestly want to go with him?"

His tone was very deliberate; and there was a sternness, too, in his eyes which she could not meet and her reply was almost inaudible.

"You wouldn't like it in France, you know."

"But what's the use when — " She glanced fearfully at the pistols covering them.

"Oh, these creatures!" he laughed. "You don't think I'm afraid of a pair of scruffy curs like them, do you?"

Caroline put up her hand to stifle a gasp of horror as he strolled coolly up to one of the men and stood within an inch of the muzzle of his pistol.

"You're very confident, my friend — too confident," Sir James drawled sourly. He turned to one of the men. "Max, fetch a rope and tie him up."

When Max had gone downstairs a strained silence fell upon the little group. Of the four the horseman appeared the least ill-at-ease. He had edged close up to the table and was standing with his hands behind his back, an amused smile on his handsome face, softly humming a little tune.

Caroline, as she looked up at him, was driven to make a last desperate appeal for him. "Oh, please don't harm him, Sir James!" she pleaded, seizing the baronet's arm. "You know you promised me that — "

"I've no time to waste now!" he snapped curtly, nettled by the other's nonchalance. "If he chooses to be foolhardy that's his affair. I've — "

The sentence remained unfinished. As Sir James thrust Caroline aside the horseman bent forward slightly and blew out the candle, plunging the garret instantly into baffling darkness. There was a crash as the table was overturned and a loud oath, followed by the heavy thud of a body hitting the floor.

"Ned, stop him, you fool!" Sir James roared furiously above the scuffling of feet.

A second later a piercing scream rang through the garret. "Let me go! Let me go! Charles, help!" Caroline shrieked in an agony of terror and pain as she fought against the iron hands which had seized her, twisting her arms behind her and bending her backwards. "Oh, you brute!"

Her voice changed to a dreadful scream of pain which died away to a pitiful moan as Max thundered up the stairs and charged into the room, a coil of rope in one hand and a lantern in the other. He pulled sharply at the sight of the strange scene which confronted him. In the middle of the floor, his legs entangled in an overturned chair, lay Ned, cursing viciously as he struggled to kick himself free. A few feet away from him, alert and unsmiling, stood the horseman, holding a pistol. In front of the window there were two figures. Sir James held the taut body of Caroline with one hand while he pressed a pistol into her back with the other.

In the feeble light of the lantern the horseman did not instantly grasp the situation, but when he did his face paled with anger and his eyes riveted on the baronet in a frozen stare.

"Not so fast, my friend! You can't escape as easily as that!" The latter laughed grimly. "Put that pistol down!" he ordered. "I warn you I'm in no mood for trifling. This lady's life will be forfeited if you try any more tricks on me."

The horseman lowered his pistol slowly and tossed it on to the floor.

"I congratulate you on your quickness." His voice rang with scorn. "I might have known you wouldn't scruple to use any means to save your skin."

"When it is a matter of life or death I'm afraid I can't afford to be chivalrous," Sir James returned imperturbably. "I underrate neither your cunning nor your audacity and I shall make absolutely certain that you don't get another chance of cheating me."

"I am obliged to you for your frankness. I shan't expect any mercy from you now."

"Oh, my dear fellow, you are under a misapprehension if you believe I intend to take your life!" cried the baronet. "When I am safely on my way to France with my young friend here I shall have no further interest in you."

"I don't understand you."

"I have agreed to let you go when we have left England."

"You're a trifle sanguine if you think I shall be taken in as easily as that."

The baronet shrugged disdainfully. "I'm not greatly concerned with what you think. If you are so unwise as to resist you will have only yourself to blame for the consequences," he warned. He turned to the two men. "Tie him to that chair. We must be on our way."

Max and Ned took hold of the horseman's arms and pushed him on to the chair just in front of Caroline. Her eyes met his for a second; then they closed and she uttered a long sigh and slumped forwards in a swoon. The sudden weight of her body pulled Sir James forward, taking him by surprise, so that for a moment he was off his guard.

In a flash the horseman was on his feet, and brushing aside the two men, he rushed at Sir James, wrested the pistol from him and hurled him against the windowledge. Jumping aside as Max and Ned flung themselves at him, he smashed the pistol butt into the former's face and knocked the latter over with a lightning swing of his powerful arm.

But the next instant Sir James was upon him, throwing his arms round his shoulders. The two men overbalanced and crashed heavily on to the floor. Locked together, they rolled from side to side, fighting desperately, till Max and Ned dashed to their master's assistance and seized the horseman's arms. He continued to struggle fiercely as they dragged him to his feet, but the odds were too heavy for him and he was overpowered. A prisoner in the grasp of the two men, who held grimly on to him, he leant, panting and dishevelled, against the wall.

"Enough of this foolery!" Sir James muttered furiously, dabbing a bleeding lip as he got to his feet. "It'll — Hell and damnation! Put that down!" he exploded wrathfully, glaring across the room.

The other three followed the direction of his eyes and the horseman uttered a boisterous laugh.

Caroline was standing in the shadows, holding a pistol in her hand. "If you move a step nearer I shall kill you, Sir James," she told him in a calm, deliberate voice.

Sir James considered the pistol pointing straight at him. "Don't be ridiculous!" he snorted irately. "Put that thing down at once!"

"I shall do nothing of the kind," Caroline stated flatly. "Tell your men to release him at once," she ordered.

"Nonsense!"

"You needn't think I'm afraid to shoot you," she warned him. "I detest you so much that I shan't have the least hesitation about killing you if you force me to it."

"That's right, Caroline! Squeeze the trigger if he so much as lifts a finger!" exhorted the horseman cheerfully.

Sir James ran the tip of his tongue over his dry lips and glowered murderously at Caroline. The intensity of loathing in her eyes and the unwavering muzzle of the pistol, much too close for her to miss, unnerved him; and while there was life there was hope; and if he did lose her it couldn't be helped so long as he got out of this devilish fix. "Curse you, you damnable little vixen!" he spat at her. "Leave go of him!" he growled to his men.

Doubtingly they released their captive who stepped quickly away from them and picked up the pistol which had been dropped in the fracas. "Now, Sir James, you will oblige me by taking yourself and your gallows cheats over to that wall," he directed in a businesslike tone, indicating the far wall with a wave of the pistol. "Get on, man!" He jabbed the pistol into the baronet's back and gave him an unceremonious shove.

Sir James swung round, his lips curled in a vicious snarl, but the steely eyes above the pistol warned him to expect no mercy if he resisted, and he walked forward to the wall, Max and Ned slouching sullenly beside him. "I'll make you pay for this yet, you two-faced, little cheat!" he ground out through clenched teeth.

When the three men were facing the wall the horseman stepped back to Caroline, and taking her pistol, slipped it into his pocket. "Ready to make a dash for it?" he whispered, drawing her back to the door.

She nodded her head, with a smile. Keeping a vigilant eye on the three by the wall, he opened the door and pushed her outside.

The next few minutes passed in a bewildering whirl for Caroline. The instant the horseman closed the door and shot the rusty bolt there was a wild scramble of boots within the garret, followed by a rain of thunderous blows on the panels of the door.

The horseman swung Caroline off her feet, tossed her over his shoulder and almost leapt down the flight of stairs; then he ran out of a door at the back of the house and down some stone steps to a narrow path where he put her on her feet again. "Come on!" he called in a hoarse whisper, grabbing her wrist.

With the sound of furious hammering, punctuated by the ominous screech of splintering wood, echoing hollowly through the building, they stumbled feverishly along the muddy path and across the yard at the front. Caroline slithered crazily on the slimy cobblestones, but the firm grip on her arm kept her from falling and they reached the lane beyond the yard without mishap.

A few yards up the lane the tall, black horse was tethered to a tree. Hearing their hasty footsteps, the animal turned its head and whinnied softly. At the same moment another sound came to their ears, the clatter of heavy boots across the yard. Caroline heard her companion curse under his breath as he swung her up on to the front of the saddle.

Before he had time to climb up behind her a man rushed upon him out of the darkness of the tree-lined lane. Turning upon his assailant who seized him by the throat, he hit him in the face with his clenched fist, sending him reeling backwards into the thick undergrowth. With a bound, he heaved himself into the saddle just as a second man came blundering up to them. He made a grab at the bridle but the horseman raised his pistol and dealt him a tremendous blow on the head. The man staggered back with a grunt, and the next instant the horse, conscious of its master's weight on its back, reared up and plunged forward, knocking the man over, and set off up the lane at a gallop.

They flew along at breakneck speed for the clattering of a horse's hooves on the cobblestones told them that they were being pursued.

Clinging tightly to the horse's thick mane, with the water from the pools underfoot spraying up into her face and the dripping branches overhanging the lane brushing her cheeks, Caroline wondered when a sudden stumble was going to send them headlong into the hedge. But the sure-footed beast sped on without faltering and in a short while they came to the end of the lane.

As they slackened speed to turn into the road Caroline clutched convulsively at the horse's mane and a frightened gasp escaped her lips for their way was barred by a man on a horse.

Her heart sank and she was beginning to despair of ever getting away from that evil spot, when, to her relief, she heard her companion hail him. "All right, Tony!"

The other man lowered his pistol and sidled his horse up to them.

"Have you got her?" he demanded in an eager voice.

"Yes; but Reddaway's after us," the horseman said. "Listen."

The drumming of a horse's hooves was plainly audible in the stillness and the two men wheeled their horses round to face the head of the lane.

"It's now or never. If he gives us the slip this time we'll never get another chance," the horseman said. "You take that side and I'll take this."

Hardly had they drawn aside when the pursuing rider came thundering up to the end of the lane. Caroline glanced up at the tense figure of her companion and she saw his right arm go up.

Then out of the darkness a voice shouted "Halt or I fire!"

But infuriated by the unexpected and frustrating check to his schemes, Sir James had lost all sense of caution. With a wild cry he reined in his horse so that it swung round sideways across the entrance to the lane and raised his pistol.

Instinctively Caroline buried her face in the horse's neck. The next moment the report of a pistol shot rang out with deafening loudness. She smelt the acrid fumes of gunpowder drifting past her face but she dared not look up in the silence that followed the shot. A moment after the scraping of hooves made her raise her head and she had a fleeting glimpse of a riderless horse careering in terror up the road, the click of its hooves resounding sharply in the eerie hush which succeeded the shot.

Then the horseman wheeled his horse round and they trotted a short distance up the road. Caroline opened her mouth to speak to him but his face was turned away from her, looking back down the road, and she left her question unasked.

In a few minutes the man whom he had addressed as 'Tony' rejoined them. He leant out of his saddle and whispered something which she did not catch in the horseman's ear; then he shook the reins and trotted off into the night.

The horseman sat listening to the sound of the horse's hooves fading into the distance. Then he looked down at Caroline and spoke to her for the first time since they had left the old house. "Tired?" he asked gently.

"A little."

"It won't be long before you're in bed," he said. "I'm afraid it's a bit far for you to go back to Ullingham Grange tonight, but I know a house just across the moor where you can stay till morning."

"What sort of a house is it?" she asked a trifle anxiously.

"Oh, you needn't be alarmed! You'll be in very respectable company, entirely female!" he assured her, with a chuckle. "I shan't be spending the night there."

She blushed and turned her head away.

He undid the buttons of his greatcoat and held it open. "Get inside there," he invited. "You'll be warmer crossing the moor."

She hesitated shyly and then moved closer to him and leant her head against his chest, and he buttoned the coat round her and, with a word to the horse, he set off again.

Nestling contentedly inside the warm greatcoat, Caroline felt she never wanted the strong arms around her to let go and she didn't care how long it took to reach their journey's end. She pressed her cheek drowsily against the smooth cloth of his coat and in a little while, lulled by the steady up and down motion of the horse, she fell asleep.

Caroline woke some time later to find herself curled up in an armchair before a cheerful fire in a cosy little room lit by candles in gleaming brass candlesticks at either end of the mantelshelf. She blinked hazily about her, at the brick-red curtains, the gay bowl of mixed flowers on the gate-leg table, the work box and pile of sewing on a stool beside the fender. Then she slid off the chair, and kneeling against the fender, stretched her hands out towards the crackling logs.

"You'll be quite happy with Mrs Joll."

The quiet voice behind her made Caroline look up with a startled expression. "Oh — yes — " She didn't know what to say. "Is she — is she your mother?"

An impish grin lit up his face. "My mother! Bless you — no!"

"Oh — I thought — " Caroline floundered awkwardly.

The horseman hovered near the door. He seemed to have something on his mind but could not bring himself to the point of speaking. "Caroline," he ventured at length, "I want to thank you for saving my life."

The lovely, grey eyes were raised to him with an expression of earnest protest. "It was you that saved me! What would have happened to me if you hadn't come?"

They gazed deeply into each other's eyes for a long moment; then he drew back abruptly and gathered up his hat and gloves. "I must go now. Tony will be waiting for me," he said.

"You're not going back to that awful place?"

"I must."

"Oh, Charles, need you?"

"Yes."

"But consider the narrow escape you've had already?"

He paused beside the door; then he came back to her, and taking hold of her hands, he looked at her intently. "Do I matter . . . that much?"

She lowered her eyes and there was a catch in her voice as she answered in the merest whisper "Yes."

His arm slid gently round her waist and he drew her closer to him. "Caroline, my darling, I love you so much!" he burst out in a voice husky with emotion. "I have been in love with you ever since that first night on the moor! Oh, Caroline, dare I hope . . . ?"

She looked up at him, tears welling up in her eyes. "Oh, Charles, dearest — yes!"

She buried her face in his chest with a sob and he laid his cheek against her curls. "Dear heart!" He lifted her head up, and bending his face to hers, he kissed her soft, red mouth, crushing her against his body in a long, fierce, passionate embrace which almost stifled her. Her head swam dizzily and she hung helpless in his strong arms, surrendering utterly to the exhilarating ecstasy in which she was submerged. They drew reluctantly apart and he said "Now that I have accomplished the task for which I was sent here I am free to return to my own home. Will you — come with me? Will you consent to be my wife?"

Her heart was too full for her to answer him at once and her lips trembled as she tried to speak. "Oh, Charles — do you mean it!" she choked out in a tremulous voice.

"Every word of it!" he declared fervently.

Tears glistened in her eyes as she nodded her head.

"You adorable angel!" he breathed in an ecstatic whisper and kissed her again. "You've made this a most wonderful night for me! I'm so happy!"

"I'm so happy too!" she murmured vaguely. "I can hardly — believe — it's — true! It all seems like — a dream!" Her voice came jerkily and she swayed in his arms. "Charles — I think — I really — am going to —"

"Caroline — no — not now!" he cried frantically, clutching her. But, her eyes had closed and she sagged limply in his arms; and when Mrs Joll returned shortly after she found him feverishly fanning Caroline's face with his hat. "She's overtired, I think," he mumbled apologetically.

"I'm sure she must be," agreed the old lady. "Never mind, she'll be better in a little while."

While Mrs Joll ministered to Caroline Charles whispered something in her ear and crept quietly out of the room.

"He asked me to tell you that he would call and see how you were in the morning," Mrs Joll explained when Caroline began to revive a minute or so later. "Now drink this glass of wine and you will feel stronger."

When she had watched her young guest eat some supper Mrs Joll took a candlestick from a cupboard and lit the candle. "I will show you to your bedroom," she said, handing Caroline the candlestick.

Caroline waited for her to snuff the candles on the mantelshelf and then she said "Mrs Joll, what is the name of this house?"

"Chollingford Hall, my dear," the old lady informed her, with a smile.

"Chollingford Hall!" Caroline exclaimed. She dropped her eyes in confusion. "Oh, I did not know!"

She allowed herself to be led to a small bedroom at the end of a long passage, where, too weary to bother any more about the mystery, she undressed quickly and was soon sound asleep under the warm bedclothes.

Chapter Sixteen

By the morning the whole countryside was fairly buzzing with the sensational news of Caroline's disappearance which it had been impossible for the Allens to keep secret, and already several explanations had been advanced to account for it. One, inspired no doubt by the vivid representation of the quarrel given by the Grange under-maids, was that she had run away. The more pessimistic-minded shook their heads gloomily and averred that she had been carried off by the Midnight Horseman.

By far the most popular supposition, however, because it combined romance with scandal, was that she had eloped with Sir James Reddaway; and it was the one Mr Allen was inclined to share when he discovered, on going to Court House to enlist the baronet's help, that he had gone away; and when breakfast time came he decided to travel south in the hope that he might glean some news of the couple at the turnpikes and posting stations which might enable him to trace them. Mrs Allen, troubled by an uneasy conscience, was strangely subdued.

Over at Chollingford Hall, meanwhile, the cause of all the upset was lying in bed, gazing dreamily up at the white ceiling above, blissfully unconscious of it all. It was broad day and the sunlight poured in through the window. Caroline sprawled luxuriously on the pillows till, she suddenly recollected, with a pang of conscience, that her aunt and uncle must still be ignorant of her whereabouts, and she scrambled hastily out of bed.

However at breakfast Mrs Joll, who was the housekeeper at Chollingford Hall, set her mind at rest by telling her that a groom had been dispatched to Ullingham Grange to inform her guardians that she was safe. Mrs Joll seemed unwilling to lose her guest yet and invited her to see over the house before she left; the temptation was too much for Caroline and she agreed to the suggestion.

After looking into a few of the principal bedrooms the housekeeper took Caroline downstairs to the dining room, and they walked slowly along the splendid room, pausing from time to time while Mrs Joll recounted some anecdote about one of the portraits, though Caroline was so enthralled by all that there was to be seen that she scarcely heeded what her guide was saying.

She had just studied a forbidding-looking gentleman with a curling, black moustache and was passing on to a lady in a panniered dress and powdered hair when a smaller portrait between them caught her eye. It was of a young man in a dark blue coat and something about his face seemed familiar to her and she turned back to it.

For a brief moment she stood looking up at the painting, a preoccupied frown on her face. Then in a flash recognition came to her and she uttered an amazed gasp. The same firm mouth, the same laughing eyes! "Who — who is that?" she jerked out in a small, bewildered voice, gazing up, open-mouthed, at the portrait.

"That is Charles Henry Landyshe, Seventh Earl of Wrosthdale," replied a pleasant voice from just beside her.

Her heart missed a beat and she spun round with a startled cry, her cheeks aglow. "Ch-arles!"

She was so astounded that she hadn't the will to resist him as he took her in his arms and kissed her. "Do you think it a good likeness?" he inquired, looking down at her with a merry smile.

"Are you really — ?"

He nodded his head. "I promised you I shouldn't fail you, didn't I?"

"I always knew you wouldn't!" she declared, with a disarming sincerity that overwhelmed him completely.

"My loveliest, sweetest Caroline!" he murmured in an ardent whisper; and lifting her off her feet, he hugged her against his body and kissed her again and again till she was almost gasping for breath.

Their lips parted slowly and she laid her head on his shoulder with a contented, little sigh.

As he looked down at her a mischievous smile crept into his face. "And did the future Countess of Wrosthdale sleep well last night?" he inquired softly.

She smiled absently. "Yes, very — " Her eyes opened wide and she jerked her head up and stared at him in consternation. "Oh, Charles — no — I can't — " She wriggled free of his arms. "Oh dear, I didn't realise — Oh, why didn't you tell me?"

"I wanted you to marry me for myself," he replied simply.

"Yes, but — Oh dear, what am I to do?" she wailed, pressing her hands to her cheeks worriedly.

"You aren't going to throw me over because I've a title! Caroline!

135

After all we've gone through together! You couldn't be so heartless!"

"No, I didn't mean to be unkind but — what will Aunt Julia say?"

"To the de — " He bit his lip. "If she objects I'll run away with you! I'll take you to Gretna!" he declared in such a resolute manner that she couldn't help laughing. "Well, do you give in?"

"Yes."

He pressed her hand to his lips. "I think I'm the luckiest man that ever lived!" he murmured humbly.

He put his arm round her waist and drew her across to a window bay and they sat down, facing each other, on the velvet cushions. Caroline's heart filled with pride and affection as she looked at him in his well-cut, buff-coloured coat, with the sunlight tinting his light brown hair with touches of gold.

She pushed back a stray lock which had fallen over his brow and slipped her arms round his neck and kissed him.

"Has Mrs Joll shown you the house?" he asked, pulling her on to his knee.

"We were going over it when you came in."

A faint blush tinged her cheeks as she recalled how he had surprised her and he grinned. "Shall you like living here?"

"Oh, Charles, shall we? Oh, yes, that would be lovely!" she cried, her eyes shining with delight; then her face clouded. "Shall we have to entertain a great deal? I mean — will there be lots of balls and dinner parties and things like that?" she asked nervously.

"Probably; but you're not frightened, are you?"

"A — little. I'm afraid you'll find me shockingly ignorant of the ways of fashionable society."

"I think that's what made me fall in love with you. You're so genuine and unaffected. You're the divinest girl a man could ever wish to marry!"

"Dearest Charles! You're very kind! I shall never feel afraid if I have you to look after me!" she murmured, nestling against his shoulder.

"A girl who can hold a pistol as steadily as you did last night need never feel afraid," he smiled.

She shuddered and was silent for a moment; then she said "Charles, did you break into Court House?"

"Yes."

"Why?"

"I thought I might find something that might be of use, letters, for instance."

"Did you?"

"I found a diary in his bureau which had in it dates of appointments with mysterious visitors referred to by initials at a spot called 'the old mill'. These appointments always took place at night. I copied them down — there were only a few — so that I could watch the rendezvous when I found out where it was. There are three mills in the neighbourhood; one is inhabited but the other two are derelict. Tony and I watched them all, and sure enough visitors called at the mill at Ocklebridge on two of the nights entered in the diary. That was how I came to be on Cullaton Moor at night. On the remaining date I had from the diary I got inside the mill and hid in the chimney in the kitchen. Later Reddaway and two other men came in and I overheard enough to prove to me that he was a Bonapartist agent."

"'Tis not surprising that Sir James was angry!" Caroline chuckled. Seeing the look of perplexity on his face, she went on to explain how Benjamin had told her about the incident at Court House. They laughed happily together; then a sudden thought crossed Caroline's mind and she turned to him in great perturbation. "But, Charles, what am I to tell them when I return home? How shall I explain what happened?"

His dismayed grimace showed that he had overlooked this problem too. "Damn, you have me there!" he exclaimed. "H'm, we'll have to think of a way of clearing that jump!" He rumpled his wavy hair, temporarily nonplussed, and pondered for a minute or two while Caroline regarded him anxiously. "I know — I'll go and see Lord Gillsburn — he's the Lord Lieutenant of the County — and I'll ask him to write me a letter for your uncle. Gillsburn's known about all this. I'll ride over to Kelligrew Castle today!"

"How long will you be away?"

"Till tomorrow morning. I'll come to the Grange immediately after breakfast. Can you manage till then?"

"It seems I have no choice," she laughed. "But I don't know what people are going to think of me."

"Tell them that Reddaway tried to run off with you and if they quiz you too much pretend you've got a headache or something."

Caroline looked at him demurely from beneath her long eyelashes, a saucy, little smile on her lips. "Would that be being genuine and unaffected?"

"No, but I'll overlook it this once," he retorted grimly, giving her curls a playful tug. "Then we can — " He stopped abruptly. "Dash it, what a fellow I am! I was forgetting!" He grasped her left hand. "Close your eyes. Go on," he commanded, when she gazed up at him uncomprehendingly. Caroline closed her eyes. She felt his fingers touch hers and a thrill of excitement ran through her body as he slid something cold and smooth along her third finger. "You may open your eyes now."

Shyly, hesitantly she opened her eyes. When she beheld the magnificent diamond ring on her finger she was spellbound. "Oh, Charles — it's wonderful!" she whispered in an awed tone, at length.

"It's been in my family for more than a hundred years. Every Countess of Wrosthdale has it." He led her over to a portrait of a young woman in a lilac dress. "Do you see? She's wearing it. She was my great-grandmother."

"She's very beautiful!" Caroline murmured admiringly.

"The Countesses of Wrosthdale have been famed for their beauty," he observed, with a twinkle, "and the Earls for their good taste." He turned briskly from the painting. "And now for Kelligrew Castle. The sooner I'm away the quicker I shall be back."

And in five minutes he was gone. To Caroline, as she made ready for her own short journey, it was like on a summer's day when a grey cloud, passing across the sun, casts a chilly gloom over the earth.

Chapter Seventeen

Caroline need have had no fears about her reception when she got home.

As she came up the steps Mrs Allen rushed upon her and flung her arms round her neck. "My dear child! How thankful I am to see you!" she cried, hugging her most affectionately. "I have been nearly demented! Oh, you wicked, wicked girl, what a fright you have given us all! I shall never let you out of my sight again!"

She hustled Caroline into the drawing room, and pushing her forcibly into her own easy chair, fussed around her with such sedulity that Caroline began to wish that she would be a little less solicitous on her account. "There is really no need, Aunt Julia!" she protested somewhat breathlessly. "I'm not in the least bit fatigued! I did not get up till after nine this morning!"

At this innocent admission a dreadful thought occurred to Mrs Allen and she suspended her ministrations abruptly. "Oh, good God, Caroline, where have you spent the night?" she demanded fearfully.

"At Chollingford Hall, Aunt Julia!" Caroline answered brightly.

"Chollingford Hall!" The note of astonishment in her aunt's voice warned Caroline that she was on dangerous ground. "Has Lord Wrosthdale returned then?"

"No — no, he is not there," Caroline replied, in perfect truth, though she made the lacing of her sandal a pretext for avoiding her aunt's eye.

"But how did you get there? Who took you?" broke in Mr Allen in a very curious tone.

Caroline went hot and cold all over. She sat tongue-tied, a blank look on her face, and an awkward silence prevailed till Harriet spoke. "Papa, let Caroline tell us all that happened to her. We may be able to understand it better when we have heard everything."

Dearly would Caroline have liked to slap her cousin for this unwelcome suggestion. "I don't know how to explain it all," she began timidly. "I'm afraid you'll find it very hard to believe. I can scarcely believe it happened myself."

"We shall do our best to believe you, my dear, you may depend upon it," her uncle assured her, settling himself in a chair opposite her rather like a large watchdog on guard. "Continue."

Caroline took a deep breath. "Sir James Reddaway tried to run away with me."

Her three listeners reacted visibly and regarded her in silent incredulity.

"Sir James! Tried to run away with you!" shrieked Mrs Allen. "Oh, good heavens, whatever next! Caroline, what are you saying?"

"But he did!" Caroline insisted vehemently. "He took me away because he hoped to force me to marry him!"

"Impossible! I do not believe it!"

Before Caroline could speak again Mr Allen intervened. "Julia, you wrong Caroline. It is quite true; Sir James did wish to marry her. He came to me only yesterday to ask my consent."

Mrs Allen was thunderstruck. "But why should he have resorted to such means?"

"I think the answer is simple. Caroline refused him."

"What! Refused him!" Mrs Allen rounded upon her niece. "Caroline, is this so? Did you refuse Sir James?"

"Yes, Aunt Julia."

"*Re-fused him*! Refused the most eligible bachelor in our circle! Caroline, how could you have been so foolish?"

"I did not like him."

Mrs Allen raised her eyes despairingly to the ceiling. "Oh heavens! Will nothing satisfy you?" she exclaimed weakly.

"My dear, I think we should leave Caroline to decide for herself," Mr Allen counselled; he turned to his niece. "Now, my child, let us have the rest of your story."

But Caroline had had enough. This was clearly not the time for explanations. "Oh dear, how my head aches!" she lamented, drawing her hand wearily across her forehead. "If you don't mind, Uncle George, I think I will go and lie down for a while," she pleaded meekly.

The ruse was successful. Her aunt and uncle displayed sympathetic concern, though the latter was not a little astonished at finding her thus unexpectedly overcome by fatigue after he had heard her protest only a few minutes before that she was not in the least bit tired, and she was allowed to go.

Caroline's headache effectively preserved her from further questions for the rest of the day. But the following morning, when the news of her return had got round, Ullingham Grange received an unusually large number of callers, as Mr Allen found to his dismay when he entered the drawing room to speak to his wife; for with Mrs Allen and Harriet there were Mrs Knox and Charlotte, Mrs Digby and Jane and Lady Heston-ffolliott, the wife of Sir John Heston-ffolliott of Sweetenham Park, and her eldest daughter. The array of waving plumes that turned upon him as he entered nearly made him turn tail and scurry out again. However, smothering this cowardly impulse, he greeted the ladies politely and sauntered over to the window to wait patiently for them to go.

"We are most fortunate in having him with us again," Mrs Knox was saying. "Such a charming young man! So affable and unpretentious! I declare I took to him at once!"

"Yes, indeed!" agreed Mrs Digby, with enthusiasm. "And 'tis splendid to think that Chollingford Hall is to be occupied again!"

A chorus of assent greeted this observation and Mrs Digby smiled happily.

"What do you think of the news, Mr Allen?" Mrs Knox asked him. "Are you not delighted?"

"News!" he repeated in a vague tone, not having paid much attention to the conversation. "What news, ma'am?"

"Haven't you heard?" Mrs Knox exclaimed in surprise. "Lord Wrosthdale is coming to live at Chollingford Hall! The archdeacon met him at the White Hart in Alnwick yesterday. Lord Wrosthdale had come from Kelligrew Castle, and hearing that he was going to the Hall, the archdeacon invited him to dinner and he spent the evening with us."

"Oh, yes, I knew he was back," Mr Allen replied, displaying a most disappointing lack of interest.

"You knew!" broke in his wife indignantly. "Then why did you not tell me?" '

"I only heard this morning."

"Sir John always deplored the way the late earl neglected the property," Lady Heston-ffolliott informed them. "Let us hope that his son will not fail to make use of the opportunities which such a fine residence affords."

"We cannot suppose that he will entertain a great deal so long as he remains a bachelor," Mrs Knox observed. "But — " she smiled one of her arch smiles, " — I cannot believe that such a handsome young man will remain unattached for long."

Mr Allen's eyebrows shot up and he glanced round, opened his mouth and then shut it again.

"Do you think — I wonder — might he not select a bride from — "

essayed Mrs Digby tentatively.

"Oh, we must not be presumptuous!" Mrs Knox laughed. "We must wait and see. There may not be any girl to his liking in Northumberland."

Mrs Digby agreed meekly.

"I have no doubt Harriet would have — " Mrs Knox repressed the urge to say 'had a chance', " — been a suitable choice," she remarked, smiling sweetly at Mrs Allen.

"Oh, Harriet will be very well where she is," the latter rejoined, refusing to be drawn.

"But should you not have liked her to have been a countess?" Mrs Knox insisted, delighted to press the idea now that there was no chance of it being accomplished. "What do you say, Mr Allen? How should you have liked a countess for a daughter?"

"I fear Harriet is not bold enough," was the bland reply.

"George, how can you speak so slightingly of your own child!" protested his wife.

"Well, what about Caroline?" suggested Mrs Digby eager to pursue the romantic topic.

This notion was received with pitying smiles by Mrs Knox and Lady Heston-ffolliott, though it did not displease Mrs Allen.

"You must remember that Lord Wrosthdale is privileged to select a wife from within the highest circles of society," Lady Heston-ffolliott pointed out.

"He said he knew Caroline," Charlotte Knox remarked casually, speaking for the first time since she had sat down.

Mr Allen trembled in his shoes, for it was evident that the others were very startled.

"Knew Caroline! But, Charlotte, that's ridiculous!" her mother exclaimed. "How could he know Caroline? He's never met her!"

"He said he had," Charlotte maintained placidly.

"How? When?" demanded Mrs Allen, puzzled but intrigued.

"I do not know. He did not say. Her name happened to come up in the course of the conversation and he just said he had met her."

Mrs Knox was furious with her daughter for not having told of this before as well as for her lack of initiative in not having followed it up; but then Charlotte had been brought up to take an interest in no one but herself.

"But I don't understand! How could they have met when he has not been in the locality?" twittered Lady Heston-ffolliott.

"There must be some explanation," argued Mrs Digby mildly. "He would scarcely have made it up."

"Oh, there has been some mistake, you may be sure!" Mrs Knox declared certainly. "He must have been thinking of someone else!"

Mr Allen could bear it no longer. "No, ma'am, there is no mistake," he interrupted, turning from the window. "Lord Wrosthdale has made the acquaintance of my niece and it may interest you to know that she is the lady he has chosen to be his wife."

The silence was awe-inspiring.

The plumes waved round upon him like a field of barley fluttered by a breeze and shuddered to a tense, terrifying stillness and eight pairs of eyes gazed at him in blank amazement.

"I beg your pardon?" queried Lady Heston-ffolliott icily, wondering whether he was drunk or raving mad.

"My niece is engaged to be married to Lord Wrosthdale," Mr Allen announced distinctly.

"Caroline?" his wife exclaimed in incredulous tones.

"Caroline."

"Is this one of your little jokes, George?"

Mr Allen shook his head slowly.

"Then why have I not been informed of this? Why has my opinion not been consulted?"

"Because, my dear, I only heard it myself a few minutes ago," he explained patiently.

"Nonsense! I don't believe it!" Mrs Knox exploded furiously, unable to restrain herself any longer.

Mr Allen shrugged his shoulders and smiled at her genially. "That does not surprise me in the least," he said, now enjoying the situation hugely. "But I thought I ought to inform you of the engagement before you wasted your time any further in making plans for them."

"Have you given your consent?" Mrs Knox demanded, clutching desperately at this faint hope.

"I have."

Mrs Knox had always scorned the feminine weakness of swooning, but at this critical moment in her life she felt she was very near to it. "But are you quite sure they know their own minds?" she persisted.

Mr Allen's eyes followed the two solitary figures wending their way slowly down the garden, with clasped hands and heads inclined fondly towards each other. "Quite," he murmured, with something of a sigh.

If he had tried deliberately he couldn't have hit upon a more effective way of breaking up the gathering. Mrs Digby was panting to get down to the town to proclaim this breathtaking piece of gossip. Lady Heston-ffolliott was so shocked — she had three daughters of her own — that she could not bear to stay in the house a minute longer. And Mrs Knox was furious with everyone and could hardly bring herself to bid the Allens a civil good morning, and she rode, fuming, back to the Rectory, refusing to believe a word of what she had heard.

But she did not remain long unconvinced. Before many months had passed she had watched her husband officiate at two of the prettiest weddings Emberhope had ever seen. And though she did her best to inveigle the secret from Lord Wrosthdale and his bride, for once she had to admit defeat; for Caroline steadfastly refused to divulge the smallest detail and Lord Wrosthdale merely smiled a dreamy smile and changed the subject when applied to; and Mrs Knox never, to the end of her days, succeeded in discovering how Caroline Berkley became the Countess of Wrosthdale.